HIGH STRUNG

A Glass Bead Mystery

JANICE PEACOCK

Vetrai Press

Lafayette, California

2016

For all the bead ladies
I know and love

BOOKS BY JANICE PEACOCK

High Strung, Glass Bead Mystery Series, Book One

A Bead in the Hand, Glass Bead Mystery Series, Book Two

Off the Beadin' Path, Glass Bead Mystery Series, Book Three

Be Still My Beading Heart, A Glass Bead Mini-Mystery

ONE

GREAT-AUNT RITA DIED two years ago on Miami's hottest day of the year. You'd think the old woman died of the heat, but she didn't live with us in Miami. She lived in Seattle, Washington, in a house she'd split right down the middle.

A month after my aunt died, a stiff white envelope arrived at the apartment I shared with my boyfriend, Jerry. It contained a letter written by Great-Aunt Rita, forwarded to me by the attorney settling her estate.

That letter would change my life forever.

Dear Jacqueline,

I've always felt a connection to you, because you and I are much the same. I know inside your tired heart is a woman waiting to start living. I'm going to help you break free. My attorney has my Last Will and Testament. In it, I have given you my house, as well as a savings account with a substantial sum of money.

Mr. Prescott can fill you in on the details. My only stipulation is this: You must live in my house and find your creative passion. I hope my gift helps you live a life you love.

You are in my heart,
Aunt Rita

Mr. Prescott's business card fluttered to the floor. Dumbfounded, I sat in the dim kitchen for a long time, staring at the card, rubbing it between two fingers. I'd been sitting there so long I hadn't realized it was dark outside. Jerry wasn't home from work yet. I was never sure if he'd come home right after work or if he'd stop at the bar to see his buddies and stumble in the door long after I had gone to bed.

Did I have the guts to call the attorney?

It was now or never.

"Yello?" said the voice on the other end of the phone.

Who answers the phone by saying YELLO?

"Uh, yes, Mr. Prescott? This is Jax—Jacqueline—O'Connell. I'm the great-niece of Rita...uh, uh..." I couldn't remember her last name. I could barely remember my own last name right now.

"Oh, yes, Ms. O'Connell. You're calling about the Rita Haglund property," he said. He did this every day. I didn't.

"I've never inherited anything before. What happens now?"

"Well, I suppose you come to Seattle, take ownership of the house, and live in it."

"But what if I don't want to move there? What if I like it here?" As I said the words, I knew they were a lie. I was tired of being in Miami, the land of pink flamingos and bugs the size of golf balls. I hated this apartment with its brown shag carpeting and harvest gold appliances, still around from the 1970s.

"Unfortunately, if you choose not to live in the house, I'm afraid I've been instructed to sell the property and donate the proceeds to charity."

Seriously, Aunt Rita put this stipulation on her house? I couldn't believe it. I saw her once a year when she'd fly out to my parents' house for a few weeks around Christmas. It was her chance to get away from the cold Seattle weather. I'd been close to Aunt Rita, but close enough for her to give me a house? It was hard to fathom. Everyone in my family described my great-aunt as a "free spirit," which was code for "an artist who never married and never had kids."

"Have you seen this house, Mr. Prescott?" I asked, hoping I could get some idea about whether this was a reasonable thing to consider.

"Yes, as matter of fact, I helped your aunt complete her trust in her living room a few months before she passed away. Since she never had children, she wanted her home to go to someone in her family who could use it to change his or her life. She chose you."

I could use a life-changing experience. "Is it nice? If someone gave you this house, would you be happy?"

"Oh yes, it's an excellent house. But it does need some renovation. In her later years she let the house fall into disrepair. Oh, and you might like to know that it is, in fact, two houses. Your Aunt Rita was a savvy lady. She had a spacious house, and she was the only one living in it. She split it and made a rental unit out of one side."

"Who's living there now?"

"The property is vacant."

"When do I need to give you my decision?"

"Officially, you have until the end of the month."

"What? That's the day after tomorrow."

"Why, yes it is. You've got some thinking to do, Ms. O'Connell."

Without saying good-bye, I ended the call.

Jerry came home later that evening and went straight for the TV.

"What's for dinner, babe?" he asked, not even looking my way.

"Seattle..." I murmured, returning the letter to its envelope and pressing it flat on the table.

"Seattle? Is that a new restaurant or something?"

"No, it's a city. Seattle, Washington." I stared out the window at the dark sky, the streetlights starting to blink on.

"Well, babe, let's order a pizza. I'm starving and the game's about to start," Jerry said, plopping into the vinyl recliner as he clicked the remote. The announcer's voice blared from the TV.

Frightened by the sound, Gumdrop jumped into my lap, staring up at me with his big green eyes. My cat thought he had psychic powers. Or, more precisely, *I* thought he had psychic powers.

"What do you think, Gumdrop?" I asked the fluffy gray cat.

"Pepperoni," yelled Jerry.

Gumdrop stared at me, trying to send me a message.

Jerry tossed the phone to me. "Thick crust."

I took the phone and dialed.

"Hello, Mr. Prescott? My answer is YES."

I tossed the phone back to Jerry. "I think you're going to have to order your own pizza from now on. Maybe you'll want to get a small one, since you'll be eating alone."

TWO

I WAS WORKING IN the studio, making a glass bead with the torch blazing, when the phone rang. I don't usually answer the phone when I'm in the middle of manipulating a molten blob of glass just inches from my face. To make things extra challenging, I can't stop twirling the hot glass because if I do, the whole thing will get saggy and out of balance. I was using both hands and most of my brain. I'd cranked the volume of my '80s playlist up to 11 on the iPod, and the giant ceiling fan hummed loudly.

As the little calypso tune played over and over on my phone, I knew I needed to answer. It was Val, and the fact that she was calling instead of barging in my front door meant trouble.

"Jax! Ahhhhgggg! Help! FIRE!" I heard the sound of the phone clattering to the ground. I jammed the bead I was making into the kiln, hoping it would be salvageable, and flicked off the torch. I ran out of my studio, through the house, out the front door, and made a quick U-turn into Val's door. As I burst in, I was immediately hit with the smell of burnt chocolate.

"Val, what happened?" I yelled as I ran toward the kitchen, a cloud of gray smoke lingering just above my head.

"Oh, Jax, it's awful. Awful!" Val said, stepping back from the smoldering oven.

"You look terrible." She was covered in chocolate from her elbows to the tips of her shiny red fingernails. Little bits of brown goo hung from her fluffy red bangs.

"What did you do? Why did you call me in such a panic?"

"I didn't think an exploding cake was a reason to call 911, so I called you instead," Val said.

"Well, you could have at least told me you weren't over here dying. I was worried one of your crazy boyfriends had come back to visit and was attacking you."

"Oh, only about half my boyfriends have been crazy. Still, I suppose that means there are a lot of crazy guys out there who are not particularly happy with me. Hmmmm...I'll have to evaluate my choice in men sometime," she said, attempting to wipe the chocolate cake batter off her face but instead adding more across her cheek.

"What were you trying to do here—make something new?" I asked, grabbing a dishtowel so I could mop up some of the mess.

"I was experimenting with a new recipe that has chocolate and chipotle peppers. I thought it would be a good combo, you know—sweet and heat—it's on every trendy menu these days."

I looked at her doubtfully.

"I don't know what happened. Maybe I put a teensy-weensy too much baking soda in the batter—I threw in a couple extra teaspoons since I added some extra peppers. I was getting ready to pull the cake out of the oven, and I looked in. All I could see was this molten lava pouring out of the top of the cake pan. Everything is cooler now, but wow, it was scary there for a minute. That's why I called you. I thought you'd know what to do, since you work with fire and molten glass."

"I'm not sure what to do, other than get a hose and spray the place down, including you."

"Don't you dare. You'll ruin the new throw pillows," she said.

I glanced over at a pile of animal print pillows with pink fur trim. No great loss if those awful things got destroyed.

"Let's take a look," I said, bending over and peeking inside the smoldering oven. "Actually, what's left in here looks okay." I jabbed my finger into the crust of the cake still in the pan.

"Ow! That's scorching hot." My hands had become used to high temperatures from working with hot glass, but this was a little more than I could handle.

I blew on the brown goop and then tasted it. So far, so good. I grabbed a wooden spoon off the counter and plopped myself down on the floor. I gingerly pulled the pan out of the oven with a dishtowel and scooped up some batter. "Yum. This is delicious. Have a spoonful."

With a not-so-graceful thump, Val sat down on the floor next to me, snatched the spoon, and had a taste. "You're right, it's super yummy. I'll have to try to perfect the recipe and see if I can make it so it doesn't explode."

"Yes," I agreed, "exploding desserts are not good. We should never, ever waste chocolate."

Fortified with spicy half-cooked cake batter, we cleaned up the kitchen. Since I resisted using the hose to clean up, Val's new zebra pillows were safe for now. Val still looked like a wreck and needed a shower.

"Why don't you get yourself cleaned up?" I suggested. "I'm heading over to Tessa's to help get her studio ready for some beadmaking demos, plus I've got to give my necklace and beads to the JOWL lady for the exhibition at Aztec Beads."

"Jowl? I don't think it's polite to say that a woman has jowls. I hope you don't say that to her face."

"It stands for 'Jewelry-makers of Washington League.' Someone thought that was better than Beaders of Washington League. Apparently they were worried people would called them 'Bowel' rather than 'Bowl'."

"Someone decided JOWL was the best choice?" asked Val, examining the chocolate gunk wedged under her long fingernails. "Whoever that was didn't understand that jowls are not something anyone should ever want to be associated with. I personally plan to never have jowls, or date anyone who has them."

Time to leave before I heard any more of Val's diatribe about jowls or other signs (heaven forbid!) of aging. I glanced at my phone.

"I've got to get out of here. Tessa hates it when I'm late." Tessa Ricci had been my best friend since kindergarten. She was punctual, bossy, and petite. In other words, she was the opposite of me in almost every way. And she was one of reasons I decided to move to Seattle. She had moved here with her husband Craig nearly 18 years ago.

I popped my head back into Val's doorway. "Oh, if the painter comes by, let him into my side of the house, so he can give me a bid on painting the kitchen."

I went out Val's front door and made the usual U-turn back into my place. I nearly stepped on Gumdrop, who was standing in the open doorway.

"Oh, Gumdrop, you're a good kitty for not running away. You do such a superb job as my guard-cat."

I'd left the front door open when I went to rescue Val, and he could have easily made a break for it. Gummie was an inside cat. He loved the idea of an adventure, but he had never actually been brave enough to go outside.

"Come on, big fella, I'll get a yummy treat for you."

I scooped him up, my arms underneath his fat gray belly as I carried him out to the kitchen, and set him down on the white tile counter. He probably shouldn't have been on the kitchen counter, but they were old and funky like the rest of the kitchen, so he wasn't going to damage them. And I washed the counters often. And I didn't really cook much. And I lived alone, so no one complained. It wasn't really that bad that he was on the counter. Really.

I pulled out a green ice cube from the cute pink plastic tray in the freezer and popped it into the cat's empty food bowl. As soon as Gumdrop saw the frozen cube of catnip, he went wild, jumping down from the counter, landing on the bowl, and skidding across the hardwood floor into the hallway. He started writhing around, licking the frozen lump, pawing at it, and pressing his furry head into it.

"Gummie, you are a little drug addict," I said, leaving him to his vice and heading to my bedroom to get changed.

I walked down the long hall of my skinny house with all of its rooms set in a straight line. The kitchen was the first room past the entry, followed by a cozy living room full of "vintage" furniture—by which I mean "used items from my dead aunt and cast-offs from friends."

Next was an office, which doubled as my guest room and had also become the overflow space for my studio. Tessa called this room the "Bead Lair," but I'd been trying to break her of that habit.

My bedroom followed, tiny but cozy, and smack in the middle of it was a beautiful cherrywood sleigh bed I'd inherited from Aunt Rita along with the house itself.

And finally, all the way in the back was my bead studio.

Val's side of the duplex was a mirror image of mine except at the back, where I had one more room than she did. My side of the duplex had a room that ran the full back width of the house, giving me a doublewide space for crafting my beads and jewelry. Working with beads full-time wasn't exactly what I thought I'd be doing with my life, but here I was, and I was happy.

In the bedroom, I looked in the full-length mirror on the back of the door. What was I going to do with myself? I was a mess. I'd been working in the studio all morning, making a few last-minute beads for this weekend's exciting events—a bead sale, plus beadmaking and jewelry classes. My usual outfit was jeans and a T-shirt, long sleeves in the winter and short sleeves in the summer. I'd promised myself I'd try and look my best for this important weekend.

The T-shirt I was wearing was speckled with chocolate, thanks to Val's culinary catastrophe. I changed into a clean top and decided jeans and clogs were going to have to be good enough for today. I ran my hands through my light brown hair—my version of combing since I'd cut it short.

No one should ever arrive at a bead event without wearing beads. I found some fun earrings, each with a purple cone-shaped bead dangling from the ear wire. I knew I'd have to try and dress better tomorrow. Val was forever after me to look nice and act pretty. Or was it look pretty and act nice? I could never remember. I wasn't particularly good at either—at least not at the same time.

I went back to the studio to get ready to go. Boxes and trays of beads were stacked in every corner, on every shelf, and even marching up the staircase to the attic. When I created jewelry, I used all sorts of pre-made beads to complement the ones I'd hand-crafted. My stash included everything from the tiniest seed beads to large silver pendants from Thailand. The studio was my creative zone, the place I was happiest—a place I could work and play, and most of the time there was no difference between the two.

This week, the chaos wasn't too bad. Since I'd had a group of Girl Scouts over last week for a jewelry-making demonstration, I'd cleaned up a little—well, a lot—before they arrived. I'd put the bits and pieces of necklaces in progress into shallow ceramic bowls to try and corral everything from each project into the same place: glass beads, silver beads, other small beads I'd purchased, a clasp, and all the other components needed to complete a necklace. Since making jewelry was less intense than handling a torch that spewed a foot-long flame, I worked on necklaces and earrings each night to relax.

The necklace project bowls ran in long rows along the table below the back windows spanning the length of the room. Those windows let in gorgeous light, even on the dreariest of days.

This had been Aunt Rita's sewing room, where she'd created stunning quilts well into her 80s. She'd left behind four massive tables with bolts of fabric stored on shelves below each work surface. The bolts were gone now, replaced by trays of beads, bundles of wire, and equipment for working with glass. On the widest table I had set up a torch, attaching it firmly to the work surface I'd covered with old kitchen tiles I'd found in the attic. They'd probably been there since the house was built at the turn of the century. Not this century, the one before it.

On the smallest table by the back door were trays of the beads I'd made, and a sample necklace made with them. Everything was packed and ready to take to Aztec Beads, the new bead store in town.

The owner, a woman named Rosie, decided she'd have a gallery show and sale featuring the work of glass beadmakers as part of a grand opening celebration. She'd added some free workshops on how to make jewelry, to entice customers to visit her shop. She hoped they'd stick around afterward to buy everything they needed to complete the projects they'd learned about in the workshops.

Rosie had teamed up with a woman named Judy, a member of the local bead society, recently—and unfortunately—renamed JOWL. Judy was coordinating the exhibition, sales, and classes at Aztec Beads. I packed my lovely red VW Beetle, the Ladybug, with the trays of beads, and headed for Tessa's glass studio. It was going to be a great weekend.

But, it didn't turn out as I expected.

THREE

TESSA, EVER THE SMART businesswoman, decided to host some demonstrations on Friday before the weekend's events at Aztec Beads. It was a great plan for getting people to come to her studio as well as to Rosie's bead shop. A few years ago, Tessa rented the perfect place in Seattle's funkiest neighborhood, the Fremont district. Fremont was known for the enormous troll that lives under a bridge in the area. It's not a real live troll, just a statue, but between that, the giant bronze sculpture of Lenin, and the wonderful eclectic shops, it was the perfect place for her glass studio.

Fremont Fire had a retail area in front where Tessa sold her own work as well as the work of other local artists. The back half of her space was the glass studio. All types of people came to the studio to take classes, use the torches Tessa set up, or learn to make a plate by fusing together sheets of glass in a kiln. Tessa was there to help the students, and of course to sell them whatever supplies they needed.

Her studio was in an edgy neighborhood, but Tessa herself was the most down-to-earth person I'd ever met. Her clean-scrubbed face and brown shoulder-length hair said "soccer mom," not artist. The funny thing about artists is that they look like normal people. In fact, I find that the people who look the most "artsy" are often people who have the money to spend on interesting clothing—and that's almost never a working artist.

I parked the Ladybug, and as I walked toward Tessa's shop, the smell of bagels wafting from the open door of The Bagelry beckoned. A few spoonfuls of half-cooked cake batter had not been a good start to the day. I stopped in and picked up a dozen bagels, cream cheese, and some coffee. Since I was juggling a sack of bagels and a tray of drinks, I pushed my way backward through the door of Tessa's studio.

"Good morning," I yelled to Tessa and her daughters. "I brought food. Tessa, here's your espresso; we've got bagels." I put the bag on the counter by the front door.

"Excellent!" Tessa took her cup and gave me a tight hug. "Are you ready for a fun weekend?"

"I think so. The big question is, are *you* ready for the demos tomorrow?" I asked, smearing my bagel with more delicious cream cheese than was necessary.

Dylan McCartney opened the door and slipped languidly into Tessa's shop.

"Hey, Tessa. Hey, Jax." Dylan never seemed to be in a hurry and was always scruffy around the edges. That comes with being a 22-year-old guy. If he'd been in Southern California, I'd have called him a surfer dude. Here in the Pacific Northwest, his T-shirt, flip-flops, and threadbare jeans looked out of place. He never looked like he was cold, but I couldn't wear so little without freezing to death when temperatures dipped to the 40s outside. Today it was 52 degrees and damp, which was typical weather for Seattle in April. I didn't want to think about how warm it might be in Miami right now.

Two heads popped out from around the corner of the storage room on the side of the glass studio.

"Hi, Dylan," Tessa's teenaged daughters said at the same time.

"Hi, ladies," he said, smiling shyly, as he pushed shaggy sand-colored hair out of his green eyes.

"Izzy, Ashley, do you want bagels?" asked Tessa.

"Not hungry," both girls replied.

"Well then, get back to work," ordered Tessa. She knew how to keep those two girls focused, which wasn't always the easiest thing to do. Izzy was 16 and had gotten her driver's license a few months earlier, much to her delight. To say that 15-year-old Ashley was jealous of her older sister's new freedom would have been an understatement.

The girls disappeared back around the corner, and I could hear squeals and laughter. I wasn't sure, but it seemed like it might have had something to do with Dylan.

Tessa rolled her eyes and laughed. She had a good sense of humor about her daughters, as did her husband, Craig. Today was going well for the girls—they weren't fighting. There seemed to be a constant battle between the two, except when their little brother was around.

Joey was four years old, an unexpected addition to the family when Tessa's daughters were 12 and 13. While the two girls fought over almost everything, they were united on this: They loved and protected Joey above all else.

It's funny, but in my family, we had the same situation. My sister Connie and I were a year apart. Our brother Andy followed Connie by seven years. I'm sure my parents were disappointed that their eldest had turned out to be an artist, and not something important like lawyer Connie or computer genius Andy.

"Dylan, do you want me to take your beads over to the shop?" Tessa asked.

"Sure, that'd be great."

"I'll grab them when I go. Thanks for watching the studio while I'm gone," Tessa said.

"No prob." Dylan was a man of few words, and a big appetite. I noticed he was already on his second bagel. Poor guy, he didn't have much money for food.

"Do you need any more help getting things set up for tomorrow's demo?" I asked.

"I think I'm as ready as I'm ever going to be. Plus, I've got some time before the demos start. You'll come for some last-minute scurrying around in the morning?" This was Tessa in her super-efficient mode; she didn't wait for a response. "Judy from JOWL wants everyone to take their inventory to her by two o'clock, so we'd better get going."

"Ashley, you promised to babysit Joey tonight. And don't forget, Rosie's son, Benny, is coming over, too. Izzy, since you don't have anything better to do, you can help your sister."

Both girls glowered at their mother and groaned in unison, crossing their arms and tipping their heads back with attitude only teenage girls can pull off.

Tessa grabbed her box and Dylan's and was ready to head over to the bead shop.

"Ashley, you come with me. Jax and I need to drop our boxes off at Aztec Beads, and then we can pick up Rosie's son." Joey and Benny hadn't spent much time together, but they were already becoming fast friends, as only four-year-olds can: shyly saying "hi" one minute, and then a moment later sharing a Popsicle and pretending to be tigers.

In her no-nonsense style, Tessa continued delegating. "Izzy, you take my car, and we'll meet you at home a little later."

A bright smile burst across Izzy's face. Ashley continued to scowl, but now it was directed at her sister. She was jealous.

"And, Izzy, get some gas, will you? The tank's almost empty," Tessa said, pressing a wad of bills into her daughter's hand as we headed out the door. "Use it all on gas—not snacks." Tessa watched as her daughter pocketed the cash.

"Sounds good to me," said Izzy, trying not to sound too excited, fearing it would make her look uncool in front of Dylan.

We put Tessa's and Dylan's boxes of beads and necklaces into the trunk with mine. Izzy pulled up next to us in the van. "Bye, Mom. Thanks for the car. I promise to drive safely."

"If you get in trouble, call me—but not while you're driving," Tessa called after her, as Izzy waved and pulled away. Even with her bossy attitude, Tessa was really just a big softie inside.

We waved as we watched the van move extremely slowly down the road and turn the corner. Ashley, standing next to the Ladybug, wistfully watched Izzy drive away in her mom's minivan. I'm not certain, but just after we couldn't see the van anymore, I heard what sounded to me like squealing tires and burning rubber.

"Good thing I put a GPS monitor on the van," said Tessa.

"What?"

"A GPS monitor. I can use my phone and track her location."

"But you can't press the brakes if she's going too fast."

"No, but I can at least make sure I know where she is." Tessa worried about her girls, like most parents do.

FOUR

"**SHOTGUN!**" shouted Ashley, as we turned to get into the Ladybug.

"Seriously, Ashley? You thought that would work? Get in the backseat," commanded Tessa.

Ashley grumbled as she squeezed herself into the back. The space was cramped back there, and tiny Tessa would have fit better than her tall daughter. But Tessa outranked her, and she slid into the passenger seat next to me.

"Next stop—Aztec Beads," I announced, as I turned the ignition on the Ladybug and we headed to the bead shop.

"What do you have for the JOWL lady?" I asked Tessa.

"For the exhibit piece, I made a necklace of black beads with polka dots in all different colors, and then I've got some disc-shaped Thai silver beads that go between each of the glass pieces. I brought two whole trays of hollow beads to sell."

"Sounds fun," I said. Tessa always had terrific new designs. During workshops at her studio, she taught people to make beads, but often those students also bought some of Tessa's own work, knowing it would be a long time before they could perfect all of the techniques she had mastered.

"And you? What do you have to sell?" Tessa asked.

"I made some white heart beads," I replied.

"Plain heart-shaped beads? That sounds a little boring for you."

"Oh, sorry. They're beads that have one color on the inside and another color on the outside," I explained. "You know, kind of like a Tootsie Pop. I use white at the center and transparent colors on the surface."

"Oh, I get it—'white heart' because it has white in the middle. I'm sure I'll love them." Tessa had been supportive of me since I'd moved to Seattle. My skills as a glass beadmaker had improved with Tessa as my instructor. And she'd brought me into her family, since mine was on the other side of the country.

"Well, let's just hope the customers love them." I needed to top up my bank account to support the next phase of home improvement: painting the kitchen. My ancient kitchen needed more than paint, but at least a new color on the walls would brighten it up. Val's kitchen had been painted a couple years ago, when I'd made it a priority to get a tenant on that side of the duplex paying rent after many long months of renovations. My side of the house was going to have to wait until I had more money under the mattress.

I parked at the curb outside Aztec Beads. Rosie had been able to rent a prime piece of real estate right in Wallingford, one of the hipper neighborhoods in Seattle. It was the perfect place for Rosie and her kids. Her shop was on the bottom floor of a two-story building. There was an apartment upstairs with a balcony. Stairs led down from the balcony onto a small patio at the back of Rosie's shop. Another set of stairs connected the apartment to an area next to the front counter inside.

The building was painted vibrant red, with a brand-new sign at the corner. The image on the sign was an Aztec figure. He was lying on his back holding a tray aloft, as if making an offering to the gods. His offering: strands and strands of beads. Aztec Beads.

"Mom? Can I go up the street to Babylon, the new music store?" Ashley asked Tessa as we parked. "They have all this cool vintage vinyl I want to check out."

"Vintage vinyl?"

"You know, like, records? Funny stuff, like, The Flock of Seagulls?" Ashley had that annoying habit, as so many teenage girls do, of ending every statement as if it were a question. Oh, and including the word "like" as often as possible.

"A Flock of Seagulls," Tessa corrected. "Jax, didn't you and I love them?"

"We did," I agreed, embarrassed. "Of course, we were both about three years old when those guys were popular." This was a lie; we were in high school.

"Yes! And remember those wacky haircuts?" added Tessa, as she got swept up in her reverie of the mid-1980s. "The long crazy bangs covering the lead singer's face," she said, trying to mimic the style by pulling all of her hair up and over to one side.

"Whatev," said Ashley, rolling her eyes and using another extremely annoying speaking style: abrevs. That is, abbreviations for any multi-syllabic words. Because it was apparently too exhausting to say "whatever."

Without waiting for a response, Ashley bolted from the car and down the street.

"We'll drive by in a little while and pick you up. Look for us, because I bet you don't want me coming in there to get you," Tessa shouted as her daughter sped toward the record shop. "And don't buy any Duran Duran albums; I've got them all at home."

Ashley cringed with embarrassment.

"Tessa, you don't want to shout that out loud," I advised her. It was true, she probably did have all of those albums. And if she didn't, then I did.

We looked down the street, and Ashley was nowhere in sight. She'd been moving quickly, trying to make a fast escape before we embarrassed her further.

As we entered Aztec Beads, we saw Rosie's daughter Tracy behind the front counter. Tracy was pretty and young, but frail, her dark eyes lacking the vibrancy you'd expect of someone fresh out of college. She should be ready to take on the world, but instead looked like she'd rather hide from it.

Tessa and I stood by the counter with our boxes of beads, trying to figure out what to do next. The place was packed. Some were beadmakers like us, milling around trying to find a place to put their beads and doing some shopping, because it was too hard to be at a bead sale without looking around for something new.

The place was also packed with beads: revolving racks of sparkling crystals in every imaginable shape and hue, vials of tiny Japanese seed beads in a rainbow of colors carefully arranged in clear plastic cubbies, thick strands of ethnic beads from all over the world, and dozens of trays of gems and pearls. All the other bits and pieces needed to make jewelry jammed the shelves and tables around the shop. It was a beader's paradise.

Next to the shop was the gallery where this weekend's show would be. The classroom was at the back of the shop.

"Tracy?" I said, trying to get her attention. She seemed to have tuned out the chaos around her. "We've got our beads. Is Judy from JOWL here, so she can check us in?"

Tracy pointed through the crowd. "I think she's in the classroom doing inventories for some of the artists," she said, more loudly than usual to make sure her soft voice carried over the din of the crowd.

Just then, Rosie broke through the crowd, hustling up to the counter by the window where Tracy stood. Rosie was a fireplug of a woman; her dark hair, complete lack of a neck, and right now the intense look of anger on her red face made her look like a very serious fireplug. This wasn't a woman you wanted to mess with. She meant business, and as far as I could tell, with all of the people buzzing around her shop, her business was doing very well.

"Tracy! Did you call the police about those two thugs trespassing on *my* property?" Rosie demanded, pointing her stubby finger toward the window at a young man and woman on the sidewalk.

"Is that Misty and Nick?" I asked Tessa in a whisper.

Tessa nodded.

The couple had spread out a colorful batik cloth on the sidewalk and had pulled out all sorts of glass beads and pretty woven bracelets. I wasn't sure what made these two people "thugs," because every time I'd chatted with them they'd been sweet. Maybe down on their luck, but they seemed like good people. Misty, the young woman, was wearing an old red flannel shirt and faded jeans. Her hands darted from item to item as she laid out the bracelets with care, the cuffs of her shirt pulled back to reveal a tiny geometric tattoo around her right wrist. Her partner, Nick, pulled off his hooded black sweatshirt and settled down cross-legged on the ground next to the cloth, his knees poking through the holes in his jeans.

Nick opened his backpack to start working on some new bracelets, engaging customers with a charming smile as they came by. From what Tessa had told me, Nick and Misty had no permanent place to call their own, and they apparently did a lot of couch-surfing.

Several people stopped to look at what they were selling, and while they didn't make any sales in the short time we watched them, it did seem like they had enough interest in their jewelry that they'd have some buyers eventually. I could nearly see the smoke rising from the top of Rosie's head as she flailed her arms around and shouted at Tracy.

Tracy tried to reason with her mother. "I don't think we can do anything, Mama. They are not on our property. It's the sidewalk, it belongs to the ci—"

"This is ridiculous. Nobody has any balls in this city," Rosie said, punctuating each word with a thump on the counter with her fleshy fist. Tracy winced each time Rosie's hand made contact. "I will deal with this—and you—later!"

Rosie turned to leave and saw us standing there, having just witnessed her outburst. She grimaced, just a little. It was enough to remind us she was human and had just embarrassed herself with her temper tantrum. Then we watched as Rosie's stout body wedged its way back through the crowd and out of sight.

Tracy looked woefully out the window. She didn't know what to do. This couple couldn't be much older than she was. Tracy clearly didn't agree with her mother, but didn't seem to be able to stand up to her. I supposed Rosie didn't like the couple cutting into her potential profits, but really, were there going to be that many fewer beads sold in the shop because a couple of kids were trying to make a few bucks to make ends meet?

"Let me help you find Judy," Tracy said, composing herself as she tucked her long dark hair behind her ears. We followed Tracy through the shop and into the classroom at the back of the building, where she pointed out Judy to us.

Judy was standing right in the middle of the room, and as people approached her, she spun around to greet them, like a middle-aged whirling dervish. She wore a tiger-stripe bead on a long chain, nearly whacking nearby people as she turned. While Judy's necklace was pretty, the rest of her needed a makeover. If Val ever met her, she'd be trying to convince Judy to let her give her a complete overhaul. Val was always looking for frumpy women to "fix," and Judy was a prime candidate, with her gaudy oversized jungle-print top.

Judy was the hardest working volunteer I'd ever met, and an extremely talented jewelry designer. This weekend of events was her brainchild. Everyone who wanted to be part of this exhibition had to apply to the Jewelers of Washington League. I agreed with Val, JOWL wasn't a good acronym. It spelled something I, and everyone else I knew, didn't want, especially when we looked in the mirror and saw our faces gradually drooping every day. But the idea for the bead-related weekend was brilliant. Artists applied to exhibit their jewelry at the event, and for those who were accepted, it was a terrific way to gain exposure and meet new clients, both professional designers and hobbyists. Unfortunately, with only one person to check in all the beadmakers, it took forever to get Judy's attention.

"Oh, hi, Tessa," Judy said, with a squeaky voice. She grabbed Tessa's hand with hers and gave it a thorough shaking.

"And you must be Jax. Nice to meetcha," Judy said, looking up over the top of her bifocals from her clipboard. Fortunately, she didn't try to shake my hand because I had a tentative hold on a stack of boxes; I wasn't sure if I could manage even a head bob without everything tumbling to the floor.

Judy was too enthusiastic for me, especially since I'd only had one cup of coffee today. She was pleased that there were so many people here to set up for the gallery show. She was the sole juror for this event; its success depended on her ability to choose the right artists to sell their beads and to decide who had appealing workshop projects. Rosie was counting on the success of this event to bring in loads of new customers, who would buy the supplies needed to complete each of the workshop's projects.

"Okay. Let's see, where's the clipboard? Oh, ha! Right here in my hand," said Judy, trying to laugh at herself. We weren't really laughing with her—or at all. We did smile with gritted teeth, but mostly because we were feeling impatient. Thin curly wisps of hair were stuck to Judy's forehead. Either she was always moist around the edges or she was having a "personal heat wave," as we sometimes said about women of a certain age—the age we were rapidly approaching.

"Jax, those are super earrings. Did you make those?" Judy said, reaching over and pulling one of them toward her so she could examine it more closely. My head followed along so she wouldn't rip the earring right out of my ear. At this proximity, I could see a million tiny droplets of sweat across her brow.

As Judy released the earring, I pulled away as fast as I could.

"I did." I figured if I kept my responses short, maybe Tessa and I could get out of here before we turned another year older.

"Right, I've got Jax," said Judy, putting a giant checkmark next to my name. "Oh, Jax, we don't have a studio name for you."

I'd never thought about an official studio name before. I'd always just used my name, Jax O'Connell, Jacqueline if I was feeling especially formal or fancy.

"Ladybug Beads," I said, knowing immediately what the name should be. It was a spontaneous decision, but it seemed like a good choice: I named my studio after my car.

I'd bought the car when I was getting ready to leave Miami. I'd gotten a huge final paycheck when I left my job at Clorox—they paid me for all of the vacation time I hadn't used. Since I'd never taken a vacation, it was a sizable sum. I took a chunk of money out of my bank account and bought a new car, having decided I

didn't need the beat-up old Honda Civic anymore. I went to the VW
dealership and bought my dream car: a brand-new red Volkswagen
Beetle with a black ragtop, which I christened "The Ladybug" with
a bottle of Diet Coke at the side of the road during my move to the
Pacific Northwest.

Judy looked up from her clipboard and focused on Tessa. "Aha!
Now, let's see. Fremont Fire. Got it," Judy said, adding another
checkmark on her list next to Tessa's name.

"We brought Dylan's beads. He's White Mountain Design,"
Tessa said.

"Okay. And a big fat checkmark for him," Judy said. "Let me
show you the exhibit area. You can set up your sample necklace on
the pedestal, and then your beads for the projects can go directly
below it, so customers can select what they want to buy for the
weekend's classes."

The gallery was beautiful, with its deep burgundy walls and
matte silver exhibition pedestals. The jewelry and beads were going
to be displayed on top of each of the waist-high columns. A broad
window opened onto the gallery, allowing passersby to look in at
the displays. Glass jewelry needs to be lit properly in order to show
off its shine and transparency, and Rosie had done a brilliant job of
making sure the lighting was perfect for the exhibit.

"You've each got a display bust to put your necklace on." Judy
was speaking so quickly she sounded like a tape recorder put on
fast-forward. The faster she talked, the squeakier she was. "We
have some other forms available if you need them—for instance,
if you have a bracelet to display. I may make some adjustments to
the displays, and, of course, we'll make sure everything stays safe
and secure.

"Jax, here is your pedestal." Judy patted the top of it and wiped
off some invisible dust, leaving a trail of moisture behind. "And
Tessa, you and White Mountain, your pedestals are right over there,"
she continued, pointing to the opposite wall.

"I'm glad you're doing this weekend of workshops," I said.

"You mean Weekend of Education, Enlightenment and Design?"

Judy sounded proud of the clever name she'd given the weekend's events.

"WEED?"

"Yes. I thought it was super. You know—our knowledge grows and spreads like weeds? I thought about WED, but I didn't want anyone to think this was a wedding-oriented event."

Instead, I thought, people will think this is a pot-smoking event. Great.

"Okie dokie!" said Judy, as she went off to find the next person on her list. Then she was gone, swallowed up by the crowd of people milling around in the shop.

"Judy needs to work on her acronyms," I said to Tessa.

"What, you don't like JOWL or WEED?"

"I can say without a doubt that both are terrible, but I bet you can't do better."

"I'm up to the challenge. How about New Ideas in Beads?

"NIB? Not good."

"Beadmakers United, Teaching Together"

"BUTT? The worst!"

"Okay, okay…so maybe it's not that easy."

FIVE

ROSIE FOUND ME a little while later, wanting to smooth things out. She'd clearly realized we'd witnessed her outburst with Tracy, and hoped to show her friendlier side. She was holding a small dog in her arms.

"This is Tito," said Rosie proudly. Tito was a tiny mutt who looked like he was part Chihuahua and part wolverine. He was all black with a white blaze across his head, right above his enormous bulging eyes. The tiny bone-shaped dog tag was the only thing adorable about this dog.

"What kind of dog is he?" I asked.

"*Mezcla*. In Spanish, it means a little bit of everything."

I reached over to pet Tito, putting out my hand slowly so he could smell it. I'm not a dog person, but I thought this was what you were supposed to do when you met a new dog.

"Hi, Tito," I said.

"RRRAAAFFF!!" barked Tito, as he snapped at my hand. Fortunately, I have fast reflexes, and was able to pull it away before he sunk any teeth into me.

"Oh, Tito, you bad, bad boy!" said Rosie, although her tone made it seem she didn't take this bad behavior too seriously. With a chuckle, she set Tito down, and he ran off and up the inside staircase to Rosie's apartment—or, possibly, to snack on the digits of some other unwary customers.

"Are you doing okay? Do you need anything?" Rosie asked with a smile, trying to continue her sweetness.

"Everything is fine," I said, as I finished setting up my pedestal.

"Oh, this pedestal is all scratched up. It looks terrible. We need to fix that."

"It's okay, Rosie. I don't mind if it has a little scratch."

"Well, I mind. Very much."

"Judy!" Rosie shouted above the crowd that was forming around the snacks and coffee Judy had brought in. "Get over here." There was no "please" in this request, tacit or otherwise, and I could hear Rosie's fingertips tapping impatiently on the top of the pedestal.

Judy came bustling over. "Yes, hi Rosie. How can I help?" Her gray hair completely flat against her head now, she dabbed at her forehead with a tissue. Judy definitely needed a break to cool down.

"The pedestal you've given Jax looks unprofessional. It's all scraped up." Rosie pointed to a faint scratch running down one side of the platform with disgust.

"It seems okay to me," said Judy with a tense smile.

I tried to back up Judy. "Yes, you know, I didn't even notice it."

"'Okay' is not acceptable," Rosie said, her voice seething with impatience.

"No one is going to notice," Judy said through gritted teeth, as she took hold of the side of the pedestal.

"It is terrible like this." Rosie locked eyes with Judy as she positioned herself on the opposite side of the pedestal and planted her feet wider.

"No, really, the jewelry is going to be fine on this display," I said as they each started pushing. I didn't want my necklace crashing to the floor if the pedestal toppled over.

"This is *my* shop, Judy, please remember that."

Realizing what she was up against, Judy dropped her hands from the pedestal. "I'll take care of this later. I've got to get back to the inventory," she said with a weak smile.

I looked down at the ground, not wanting to make eye contact with Rosie. She had come over to show her congenial side, but she'd only made things worse. Rosie didn't play well with others. I glanced up, and she strained to paste a smile on her face.

"You'll take care of the pedestal with Judy later?"

"For sure," I said, with absolutely no intention of doing any such thing.

Rosie stalked off.

SIX

TESSA AND I FOUND Tracy a few minutes later, in her usual spot at the front counter.

"Does Benny still want to have a sleepover tonight?" asked Tessa.

"It's the only thing he's been talking about all morning. He's ready and waiting upstairs. I'll go get him," Tracy said. She headed up the inside stairs into the apartment.

Moments later, Benny came down the stairs, his little red rolling suitcase, covered in cartoon cars, bumping right behind him. Tracy followed him down, carrying a similarly decorated sleeping bag and a car seat. Benny was an absolutely adorable child, all pink cheeks and wavy blond hair. Someday he'd be a real lady-killer. For now, I was swooning from his cuteness.

"Hi, Benny. I'm Joey's mom. You remember me?" said Tessa, as she knelt down to his height. Benny stood back, staying close to Tracy as he watched Tessa uncertainly.

"I 'member," Benny said.

"Great. Do you want to come to my house to play with Joey? This is my friend Jax, and she's going to give us a ride. Okay?"

We all held our breath, waiting for Benny to decide if this was okay with him.

"Yep," said Benny.

And with a simultaneous sigh of relief, we all headed out the door with Benny and his gear. After 15 cuss-filled minutes trying to figure out how to install Benny's car seat in the back of the Ladybug, we were off. We stopped and picked up Ashley at Babylon. She slithered into the backseat next to Benny. He looked up at her expectantly, and smiled. Until that moment, Ashley looked glum, knowing, I'm sure, that her older sister was out driving around alone in her mom's van, while she was stuck in a car with a small boy and a couple of middle-aged women. But when Benny smiled at her with his sweet grin, full of all those lovely white baby teeth, his green eyes glinting in the sunlight, Ashley couldn't resist.

She grinned back at Benny.

"What'd you buy?" Tessa asked.

"I got a record by Abba and one by Aerosmith."

"Those are pretty diverse choices," I said. About the only thing those two bands had in common was that they both started with the letter "A" and they were both famous in the 1970s. Ashley seemed thrilled with her purchase.

"So, how are you going to play them?" I asked.

"Oh, well, yeah. I didn't really think about that," Ashley said. "Mom, do you still have that old record player?"

"I do," said Tessa, "but I think it needs a needle."

"A needle?" Ashley looked puzzled. She was used to technology, full of tiny microprocessors and hard-drives. To her, playing CDs, let alone records, seemed old-school.

"Yes, back when dinosaurs roamed the Earth—" Tessa jokingly began.

"Yah, right, Mom, I get it," Ashley said, having heard this speech before.

When we got to Tessa's house in Ballard, her minivan was sitting in the driveway. I was glad to see that Izzy, and the minivan, had made it home in one piece.

"Don't forget about your 'date' with Allen tonight," Tessa said, getting out of the car.

"First, it is not a date. Second, I have not forgotten," I said. "See you tomorrow morning. I promise to be early."

I headed home to get ready for my "not a date."

I'd promised Tessa that Allen Sinclair could interview me. He was one of the lifestyle writers for *The Seattle Times* and was writing an article about glass beadmakers in Seattle. I'd invited him over to my house so he could see the studio, and I planned to give him an introduction on using a torch to make beads. When we'd talked about it earlier in the week, Tessa had assured me that Allen wasn't an ax-murderer.

"He doesn't look like he has ever murdered anyone with an ax," said Tessa.

"Well, just because he doesn't *look* like an ax-murderer doesn't mean he's *not* an ax-murderer. I mean, I'm sure there have been actual ax-murderers who didn't look like ax-murderers," I said, trying to be logical about this.

"Can you stop talking about ax-murderers? You're giving me the creeps."

"You brought it up," I said. In the week since that conversation, I'd been reading some of Allen's articles on the *Times* website. I'd also been doing some searching, trying to find pictures of him online (known as ogling, instead of Googling).

I did my best to pick out something for the interview that would look nice, rather than my usual jeans and T-shirt. I wanted to come across as professional, but also artistic. Usually I end up just wearing black. That way, I don't have to worry about matching, and the dark color minimizes those extra pounds of "studio butt" I've accumulated from sitting down every day working at the torch. Today's ensemble: black jeans and a black tank top. I added a pop of color with a lime green cotton cardigan. For the interview with Allen, I picked a short necklace made of nine flat lime-green beads covered with black squiggles and dots. It fit perfectly at the neckline of the sweater.

I did a quick scan through the house to make sure it looked okay, since Allen would be arriving soon. I washed a few dishes, grumbling that someday I'd have a new kitchen with a dishwasher, and cabinets I didn't have to duct tape together to keep from falling apart. At least I had decorated them with cute zigzag-patterned duct tape. Then I wandered around, doing those things people do when waiting for someone to arrive. Plumping the pillows on the vintage green velvet sofa. Straightening the framed watercolors my nephew had painted. Putting out the ingredients for drinks later, in case he wanted one. Picking up a piece of cat hair. Picking up another piece of cat hair.

Allen rang the doorbell at seven o'clock. Right on time. I really had no idea what to expect. Googling had not turned up much in the way of photos, other than the official one on the *Times* website. In that picture he was handsome, but it was hard to tell how many years out-of-date it was. For all I knew, the guy on the other side of the door would be 70 years old with a potbelly.

The person who stood on the doorstep pleasantly surprised me. Allen was on the shorter side, but at least taller than me. He had curly brown hair, dark brown eyes, and the most terrific smile ever, revealing a set of teeth that must've cost his parents a fortune in orthodontia. He was wearing a tweedy jacket, a white button-down shirt, cords, and some stylish leather boots. I always like to check out people's shoes. You can learn a lot about a person by looking at what they wear on their feet. Me, I usually stick to clogs in the studio, Mary Janes for dress up, and sneakers the rest of the time. I'm not sure what that says about me, other than I'm practical and like to be comfy. But, for Allen, his footwear meant he cared about how he looked, and he didn't mind spending money to buy something that truly pleased him. He looked a little preppy, but that wasn't the worst thing he could've been. For instance, he might've an ax-murderer... but I doubted it. He was older than me, I thought, by a couple of years.

I realized I was so busy assessing him that I hadn't invited him in. I just stood there with my hand clutching the doorknob. Allen made a slight move toward me, figuring, I suppose, if I wasn't going to invite him in, at least I wouldn't stop him from barging in. That small movement helped me gain enough focus to remember what I needed to do next.

"Oh, please come in!" I said, hoping he hadn't noticed my momentary lapse of graciousness.

"Are you Jax? I'm Allen Sinclair," he said. "Unfortunately, it's just me tonight. My photographer called in sick. I'll have her get in touch with you so we can get some shots for the article."

Allen stepped inside. "Okay, let's see." I was flustered. I felt like I didn't know what to do in my own house. Should I offer him a drink? Should I see if he needs to use the bathroom? Should I give him a tour?

"Okay, let's see," I said again, feeling like a record stuck in a groove. My palms were sweaty, and I ran them down the front of my jeans. Now wasn't the best time to start having hot flashes. I was pretty sure it was just nervousness, and not hormones.

"Would you like something to drink? I could make you a cocktail, but unfortunately, I can't have one until after I show you a bead-making demonstration. Even a tiny amount of alcohol ruins my small motor skills." I realized I was babbling, and couldn't seem to stop. "But if you—"

"I'm fine, thanks," Allen said with a smile. "Perhaps we can both have one after your demo."

His smile helped calm me down. He seemed kind, and that was a good start.

"Down this hall at the very end is the studio. Let's head on back," I said, feeling more confident.

We entered the studio, and I was glad I'd spent time to clean it up last week. My workspace looked professional, not in utter chaos as it usually was.

"Let me show you around," I said.

"Do you mind if I record you? It'll help me with the article," Allen said, pulling out a tiny digital recorder from his pocket.

"That's fine," I said. I shouldn't have been surprised by his request, but the thought of Allen listening to our conversation later did make me a little anxious. He turned on the device, pressed Record, and placed it on the table next to me.

I pulled out some trays of beads. The best ones were sitting at Rosie's right now, but these would give Allen an idea of what I made.

"These are the beads I make using a process called lampworking."

"*Lamp* working? I don't see any lamps," he said, looking around the studio.

"Early glass beadmakers didn't have the high-tech torches we use today that are powered by propane or natural gas, and oxygen," I explained. "Instead, they used an oil lamp and bellows to make a flame that was hot enough to melt glass."

"Is it the same as flameworking?"

"Exactly, and sometimes you'll hear it called 'torching,' although that isn't my favorite way of describing the process." To me, "torching" sounded like what an angry mob of people with pitchforks would do once they reached the door of a bad guy's house in one of those old movies.

"I'll give you an overview of what I've got here in the studio," I said, looking around and trying to think of an organized way of presenting information to someone who didn't know a thing about a topic with which I'm deeply knowledgeable.

I brought him over to the workbench.

"This is a torch attached to the table. It's called a Minor Bench Burner. It gets hot—I mean extremely hot, over 2,000 degrees, which is why I can melt glass with it. See these long hoses? This one attaches to the house's natural gas line." I turned the lever to open the gas line. I was happy I'd spent the money to have natural gas piped back to the studio. It meant I didn't have to bother with propane tanks.

"Natural gas—isn't that dangerous?" asked Allen. "What if it leaks?"

"Natural gas has no smell, but an odor is added to it so you can tell if there's a leak. Anyone who works with it, or with propane, knows that if they smell skunk, it is likely a gas leak."

"What do you do if that happens?"

"Turn off the gas, open the doors and windows, and get out of the building quickly if the room is filled with it. In a worst-case scenario, a whole studio can go *kaboom!*"

I'm sure I'd startled Allen at this point, and he looked around the studio casually to locate the closest exit.

"Here's the oxygen tank that, along with the natural gas, gives the torch a super-hot flame." I turned the knob on the tank's regulator to pressurize the hose that fed the torch.

"And here's my kiln," I said, flipping its switch to the ON position so I could demonstrate how it heated up to a toasty 940 degrees.

"Now, over here is the glass I use," I said, leading Allen to the stacked tubes full of different colored, pencil-thin glass rods that lined both sides of the table. "They come in a zillion different colors, both transparent and opaque. The colors of glass are amazing, and the combinations you can put together are endless."

"I can't believe there are so many colors." Allen bent down to get a closer look at the sticks of glass. "How do you choose what to use?"

"It's a challenge, but it's also part of the fun. Why don't you go ahead and pick a few different colors, and I'll use them to make some beads for you. Okay?"

Getting visitors excited about glass by allowing them to choose their own colors always worked for the Girl Scouts, and I hoped it would work on grown-ups, too.

"Wow, a challenge. How do I pick?"

"I'd pick—"

"That was a rhetorical question," he said, while he studied the colors. "I'll pick purple, blue, and green," he decided, pulling out a couple of glass rods in each of those colors and handing them to me.

"Nice choice."

"My favorite colors," he added with a smile.

"Mine, too," I admitted.

"Here," I said, trying to ensure that this would be successful demo. "Let's also pick some basic neutral colors that will help us make good beads: black, white, and clear."

I wasn't looking forward to this next part. "Now, we have to protect our eyes. These are called didymium glasses, and I wear them to help me see the glass in the flame while I'm working." I handed a pair of ugly horn-rimmed glasses to Allen, and I put on a pair, too.

"My dad had a pair like this when he was in the army," Allen told me. "He said that all the men called them BCGs, also known as 'birth control glasses.'"

I'd called them that myself, and was hoping I didn't look too terrible in them. Allen didn't look half-bad in his nerdy glasses. His dad had evidently found someone to make babies with, so his BCGs didn't seem to have caused him much of a problem.

I decided to move right along, because I certainly didn't want to talk about birth control with a guy I'd met only a few minutes ago. Allen was cute, with or without BCGs.

"The first thing I do is to light the torch, like this," I said, turning the red knob to start the flow of gas and using a metal striker to make a spark. "The torch has a yellow flame at this point, like you'd see from a cigarette lighter. I'll add some oxygen to increase the temperature." I now had a fierce eight-inch blue flame flowing out the front of the torch.

"Amazing."

"This is a metal mandrel I wrap glass around." I showed Allen a foot-long metal wire covered at the tip with bead release.

"Now, I'll take this glass rod and slowly start to put it in the flame. The glass will start to heat up and turn orange and start glowing. Then it will become soft enough that I can work with it."

"Jax, this is so exciting," Allen said.

"You clearly need more excitement in your life," I said with a laugh, hoping it didn't sound too flirtatious.

Allen laughed as well. At least I knew he had a good sense of humor.

"Once I have a bubble-gum-ball-sized blob of molten glass, I wrap it around the mandrel. I can use this tool called a marver, which is a flat piece of graphite, to smooth out the glass by rolling the bead back and forth along it, like this."

"It's kind of like a little ironing board." Allen was standing right behind me, bending down to see what I was doing. He felt very close — too close. I hoped I didn't smell too much like burnt chocolate cake.

I continued making the bead, rounding it out and adding some spirals and squiggles before completing it. It was a good bead, and a type I'd made hundreds of times over the last few years—cobalt blue with twists of purple and green swirling through it.

I was glad Allen hadn't distracted me too much. It would have been embarrassing to make a terrible bead while I was trying to impress someone.

"Bravo!" Allen said, applauding.

I smiled, glad he was such an enthusiastic audience. "And now the bead is almost done. I'll just put it right here in the kiln." I turned off the torch and quickly removed the BCGs. No need to leave those on a minute longer than necessary.

"You put the bead in the kiln to dry?" asked Allen.

"To cool down. It's far too hot right now. If I left it out on the counter, it would cool down too quickly and crack into pieces."

"Oh, like when I put cold water in my wife's expensive glass coffeepot while it was hot and broke the bottom out of it?"

A wife. Dammit. I thought maybe this guy might be some serious dating material. But I drew the line at married men. Well, at least I'd still get a nice article out of it.

"Yes. Like that. Exactly. Your wife must have been pretty mad," I said.

"Oh, yes. She had all sorts of terrible things to say about me, and my stupidity."

"Ah, I'm sorry—"

"Guess that's why she's my ex-wife now."

"What? Oh!" I said, using all of my best words in a very articulate way. I was relieved to hear he wasn't married, but it was time to change the subject before we spent any more time discussing his marital status.

"Would you like to have a drink while we finish the interview?"

"Sure, that would be great. If it's not too much of a hassle," Allen said.

"Well, it is not going to be much of a hassle for me, because you get to make them. You know how to make a mojito?"

"Absolutely. I was a bartender back a few years ago before my newspaper career took off," Allen said.

"Fantastic. I need to program the kiln to cool down overnight. If you wouldn't mind starting the drinks," I said as I pointed him back toward the front of the house, "I'll be right there. Most everything is already out on the counter."

"Where's the mint?" Allen yelled from the kitchen.

"In the upper part of the fridge," I yelled back.

"Okay. Got it," I heard him say, and then he said something else. I wasn't sure what, but it didn't matter; I was on my way.

When I reached the living room, Allen had just finished making the drinks and was walking carefully toward me with two full glasses.

"Wonderful," I said as we sat down next to each other on the sofa, another thing I'd salvaged from Aunt Rita. Was Allen sitting extra close? Or was this just the normal way people sit next to each other? I was glad I'd cleaned the cat hair off the couch before he arrived. The velvet sofa was a cat hair magnet.

Gumdrop came cruising into the room. He doesn't like strangers, and usually made himself invisible when someone came to visit. I was surprised when Gummie started rubbing against our shins as we clinked glasses and took our first sips.

"Delicious," I said. It was the first moment all day when I'd felt like I could relax. I took a deep breath and released. Ahh.

"Hard day?" asked Allen.

"Eventful," I said, sounding mysterious. I decided Allen didn't need to hear about the exploding chocolate cake or the middle-aged lady drama at Aztec Beads.

Allen seemed like a great guy. He'd enjoyed seeing the studio and my work. And, he made a delicious mojito. I was sure Val would approve of him. Gumdrop jumped up on the back of the sofa and was rubbing his head against my shoulder.

"Gumdrop. You weirdo! Go away," I said. "He's never like this," I added apologetically.

The disaster happened so quickly I didn't have time to prevent it. *Gumdrop launched himself into Allen's drink.*

He was like a cartoon clown leaping from a diving board into a Dixie cup of water. Allen dropped his glass into his lap, or more accurately, Gumdrop knocked it out of his hand. It was hard to tell what was happening—a frantic blur of gray cat and minty cocktail splashing everywhere.

Gumdrop was writhing in Allen's lap.

"I am so sorry. Very sorry. Really, really sorry." I sprinted to the kitchen for a towel. Allen was a sticky wet mess. Gumdrop was covered in liquid and continued to writhe around.

"I just don't know what's happened to my cat. It's like he's on drugs or something." On drugs. Oh dear.

"Allen? The mint you used for the mojitos. Where did that come from?"

"Oh, just like you said, in the top of the fridge. I didn't see any in the fridge, but your freezer is up there, too, so I thought maybe I misunderstood what you meant. And sure enough, you are so clever to make those little mint ice cubes so you always have fresh mint available. We used to do that at the bar—"

"You used the mint in the freezer?"

"Yes."

"In the pink ice cube tray?"

"That's right."

"Okay, well, that explains it. You see, Gummie here," I said, removing the sticky cat from Allen's wet lap, "likes catnip. A lot."

Allen, his mouth half-open, stared at me in shock and tried to focus. I was holding a soggy feline who was wriggling and now trying to get to the other glass of catnip-laced mojito.

"I'll be right back," I said as I ran with Gumdrop, holding him out from my body as far as possible, to the bathroom. I tossed him in gently, closed the door, and trotted back into the living room. Allen was standing now and staring down at his brown corduroys, which were soaked, with little bits of catnip and gray cat fur smashed into the fabric here and there.

Allen looked in horror from his pants to me. He still hadn't put it all together.

"I keep a special supply of catnip in the freezer for Gumdrop in those little ice cube trays."

Allen continued to stand there, dripping, holding his arms away from himself awkwardly so he didn't have to touch his sticky hands to his shirt.

"You just didn't see the real mint in the messy fridge. And that is totally understandable," I said, trying to make sure he understood this wasn't his fault. Even though it *was* his fault because he didn't followed my instructions. Of course, it was also my fault, because I'd let him loose in the kitchen to make our drinks unattended.

"Well, Allen, let's get you out of these sticky pants," I said, reaching across the coffee table for his buckle.

Allen jumped backward away from me. It was probably not a wise move—making me seem like all I wanted to do was take advantage of the situation by helping him remove his clothes.

"I think I'll be leaving my clothes on for now, thanks. What I'd really like to do is go and wash up, and I'll be on my way."

Allen started to walk toward the bathroom.

"Allen?" I said, cringing. "You don't want to go in the bathroom. Gumdrop is locked in there right now."

As if on cue, Gumdrop let out an ear-splitting psycho-kitty yowl from behind the bathroom door. Allen adjusted his course. He was now headed for the front door, his feet shuffling across the floor, legs apart so he looked like a gunslinger at high noon—a wide stance, arms held out from his body, ready to draw his gun.

"You know, Jax, it has been a lovely evening," Allen said, now trying to act like this sort of thing happened all the time. He was pretty unconvincing, because he was saying it through gritted teeth.

"Let me know if you need any more information for the article."

"I'll be in touch." And then he was gone.

It was a lost cause. Things had been going so well, and *boom*, in a moment Gummie had ruined everything. I mopped up as well as I could. Fortunately for the sofa, most of the drink had landed on Allen. Unfortunately for me, I'd lost the great article Allen was going to write and a possible boyfriend, too.

As I padded down the hall to my bedroom, I remembered poor Gumdrop locked in the bathroom. I opened the door and he came out slowly, looking around to see if he was in trouble. I thought he'd be a sticky mess like Allen, but it looked like Gummie had spent his time in exile cleaning himself and gleaning every bit of catnip from his fur.

I picked up the big gray fluff-ball and hugged him tightly to my chest. He had the faint smell of rum. "I'm going to change your name from Gummie to Rummie," I said to him as we headed down the hall to bed.

SEVEN

I WOKE UP TO the sound of *dingdongdingdongdingdong*.

I was going to murder whoever was ringing the doorbell so insistently, and so early in the morning. I caught a glimpse of the kitchen clock as I headed for the door. Seven in the morning! Who would *dare* ring the doorbell so early in the morning? I figured it was Val, because most of the time it *was* Val. Maybe Val had come and brought me something lovely she'd made for breakfast—although with her constant recipe tinkering, there was no guarantee it would actually be edible.

I yanked open the front door. It wasn't Val.

"Oh, Marta! Wow. You...are...HERE." Dammit. I had forgotten Marta was spending the weekend with me.

"Hi, Jax," said Marta, as she stepped inside. "Sorry I rang the doorbell so many times—I wasn't sure if you heard me," she said sheepishly.

"That's okay, I needed to wake up anyway," I lied, subtly scratching my backside.

I'd only met Marta a couple of times before at the glass bead-makers' annual conferences. She was coming in from Idaho for the weekend's events and had asked if she could stay with me. Other than being about my age, she wasn't much like me—all squeaky clean and sporty, wearing her coordinated sweat suits, like she was ready to go for a jog or play a game of rugby at a moment's notice. Even though I didn't know her well, I felt like I knew her well enough that she wouldn't murder me in my sleep.

"How was your trip?" I asked, trying to be welcoming. I seriously couldn't remember why I had said yes to having her as a houseguest. I live alone for a reason, and frankly, I hadn't had a good night.

"It was hard getting all packed up to come," she said. "And, it took a long time to get here because I had to make a bunch of stops for Stanley."

"Stanley?" I wasn't looking forward to the answer.

"Oh, yes, Stanley. He comes everywhere with me."

"And Stanley is…" I continued, hoping she would complete the sentence.

"Oh, he's my animal companion," she said with a broad smile.

"Pet?"

"Yes, well, we try not to use that demeaning term anymore."

"Dog?"

"Of course."

"And where is your animal companion staying this weekend?" I asked, because he wouldn't be staying at my house.

"Oh, I thought you knew about Stanley. I planned on him staying here with me. He is the sweetest dog you will ever meet. He won't be a bother, I promise."

I looked at her blankly. My own animal companion was going to have a kitten (although anatomically impossible for a variety of reasons) if another animal of any kind entered his house. I was sure Gummie considered this his house, and that he let me live here simply for his own convenience, because I knew how to open cat food cans.

"Well, you see, Marta, my cat, Gumdrop, he doesn't really like dogs."

"Oh, you'll see, they'll be fine. Stanley loves everyone."

But that wasn't the side of the equation I was worried about.

"Well, I'm sure we'll get it figured out," I said.

Marta popped out the front door to get her dog and her bags.

I pinched the bridge of my nose and closed my eyes, sighing deeply, hoping to clear my head and focus.

When I opened my eyes, Val was standing in the doorway, holding two cups of coffee. I jumped when I saw her—how could she have been so quiet? She handed me a cup.

We watched Marta as she struggled with her luggage. "She brought her dog," I said.

"She. Did. Not! How could she not have mentioned something as important as that?"

"No idea why she didn't think to tell me. It's going to be World War III at my house between Stanley and Gumdrop."

"Stanley. That's a cute name for a pet."

"Not a pet, Val. An *animal companion*."

"I don't get it." Val gave me a squinty, puzzled look. "Well, you know, Gumdrop always has a place to stay at my house, honey. Ever since Ken moved out, it's been lonely over here."

"We may need to relocate Gumdrop for a couple of days," I agreed. "I'm not sure if it will work any other way. Sort of uncool she didn't tell me ahead of time." I was feeling grumpier by the minute. "I'll bring him over if it looks like we're headed for disaster."

"Okay, my little human companion," said Val, taking a sip of coffee and patting me on the head. "I do not want to be around for Stanley and Gumdrop's meet-and-greet. See you around seven so we can go to the wild party."

"Val, we're going to the opening reception of an exhibition at a bead shop. The owner said anyone who wanted could stay late and have a party afterward. But, I don't think it will be 'wild'—more like 'mild.'"

"There will be guys there, right?" Val asked. Val acted more like 19 rather than 39, her real age, though she'd never admit it. The only reason I knew was because I'd peeked at her driver's license. I wanted to prove to myself she wasn't "in her early 30s," which is what she told almost everyone she'd ever met, at least for the couple of years I'd known her.

"Val, what about 'bead show' and 'bead shop' do you not under-stand? Mostly it's going to be women—bead ladies like me. Over 40—like you."

"I'm not 40 yet," she huffed, as if I had insulted her greatly.

"You might find a couple of guys there, but I wouldn't get my hopes up if I were you."

Poor Val had been through dozens of boyfriends, the most recent one—Ken, as cute as Barbie's plastic boyfriend—having moved out just weeks ago. Val had discovered the pockets of his jeans filled with cocktail napkins with phone numbers and lipstick smudges on them. When she'd confronted him with the wad of paper evidence, he'd shrugged, grabbed his duffle bag, and was out the front door in less than 30 minutes. Ken hadn't been there long, so he didn't have much to take with him when he left.

Too bad Val couldn't look at what was on the inside of someone, and not just the packaging. She might actually find someone worth-while if she did. I tried to tell her this over and over, but she never seemed to hear me.

Marta came bustling up the walkway toward me—being dragged by a basset hound would be a more accurate description. Stanley's low-slung white-and-brown body burst past me. His paws skittered across the entryway tile as Marta dropped her bags in the hall and tried to control her dog.

"Oh my gosh! Oh my! Stanley! Off! Off!" shouted Marta. "Sit! Stay!"

Amazingly, Stanley obeyed. It was hard to imagine having a pet that actually did what you told him to do. Gumdrop didn't have this skill. In fact, his skill was to do the exact opposite of what I wanted him to do. And unfortunately, reverse psychology didn't seem to work on him.

"Let me show you where your room is," I said, trying to be as hospitable as possible, but feeling like telling her I'd contracted a terrible contagious disease and that she simply couldn't stay here. It seemed too late to be making excuses.

I tried to muster some enthusiasm. "Here's the guest room. The bathroom is down the hall, right before you get to the studio at the back." I was glad the office-cum-guest room was in good shape, and not too messy. Since I'd had my laptop set up in there, I'd been trying to keep the space from getting too chaotic. I'd squeezed an elegant wrought-iron daybed against one wall. It was a splurge because I'd actually paid for this piece of furniture, along with a desk, at a local garage sale.

Stanley went wild, smelling everything in sight. He snuffled at the Oriental rug, and the tags on his collar jingled loudly as he moved around the room, his nose sweeping every inch of the floor. His tail wagged wildly, knocking the stained glass lamp off the nightstand. I caught it before it hit the floor. I was sure the dog had sensed Gumdrop and was determined to find him.

I grabbed my laptop, since I'd need it at some point this weekend and didn't want to leave it in the room. "I'll go get your bag." I eased my way out of the room and shut the door, in hopes I could contain Stanley in the guest room. I grabbed Marta's bag and noticed the front door was open.

"Gummie?" I said, as calmly as possible. I peeked out the door. "Gummie?" I called. "Oh, Gumdrop, today is not a good day for you to decide to be brave and explore the outside world."

Should I shut the door and hope he was still inside? Or did I leave it open in case he decided to come back in? Oh dear. I peered outside, hoping I could spot him, but he wasn't there. I gently closed the door, praying he was still inside, hiding in a closet.

Marta came out of the bedroom holding Stanley by the collar. The dog was panting heavily, drool dripping from the corners of his droopy mouth.

"So, Stanley—that's a cute name for a dog," I said, trying to make idle chitchat while giving her a tour around the house.

"Well, it's not his real name, just his nickname. He's a purebred basset hound. I've been breeding them for years. Jax, I'd like you to meet Ellison's Post Falls Sherlock Stanton."

"Sherlock?"

"Oh, yes, I'm an avid mystery fan," Marta said. "I especially like the ones with dogs in them." This was no surprise to me.

· "Since I'm a breeder, I get to choose his official name. But he's usually just called Stanley," Marta added.

I wasn't sure what the protocol was for meeting a dog, but I certainly hadn't done it right when I met Tito yesterday.

"Uh, hi," I said to Stanley, whose full name bordered on ridiculous.

"Say 'shake,'" Marta whispered in my ear.

"Shake?" With that, Stanley lifted his fat paw, pad-down like royalty, for me to greet him properly. I swear, this dog had better manners than I did. I gave his fat paw a squeeze, and he set it back down on the floor.

"Oh, look at his pretty collar," I said, noticing the elaborate jewelry around the dog's neck, his silver nametag tucked in among crystals, charms, and tiny glass dog bones.

"Thanks, they're my specialty," she said. "Jax, I am so sorry Stanley startled you."

"Well, it's just that I can't seem to find my cat."

"Oh, he'll turn up. When he does, you'll see that he and Stanley will be the best of friends."

"Okay, we'll hope so," I said, scanning the room, looking for a fluffy gray tail sticking out from under a piece of furniture. I didn't see one.

Marta smiled and looked like she needed to break some bad news. "One itty bitty thing I should warn you about, Jax, is that Stanley has a leather fetish."

I didn't want to think about what kind of weirdness that was.

"He likes to chew on shoes, especially fine leather," Marta said, reacting to my puzzled look.

I reached down slowly and picked up my nice leather handbag from the floor, and set it on the kitchen counter.

"I should take my cutest puppy-wuppy out to the backyard to do his piddle," Marta said.

"Piddle?"

"Oh, you know, go to the bathroom," she explained. "Don't worry, I'll clean up any messes he makes."

"I don't actually have a backyard. I have a place to park my car at the entrance to the studio back there—no real yard per se, just a cute little brick patio with a bistro table."

"Oh, well, Stanley can poop just about anywhere," she said, reassuring me.

I wasn't reassured. I was worried. Worried Gummie would never return while that dog was here. Worried about what the studio entrance might look like after several days of "piddle."

I searched for Gumdrop as I headed back to the studio. I couldn't find him anywhere. I hoped, since he was such a scaredy-cat, he hadn't bolted out the front door. Once I was dressed, I headed off to Fremont Fire, praying Stanley and Marta wouldn't destroy anything while I was gone.

EIGHT

WHEN I GOT TO FREMONT FIRE, I spotted Tessa at a table on the raised platform that would be used for the day's beadmaking demonstrations. She'd moved some of the worktables aside to make room for the rows of seats the girls had set up yesterday. It looked like an official classroom. On each chair, Tessa had placed a brochure promoting the upcoming classes at her studio. Clever, clever Tessa, always marketing her services and products.

"Where the heck have you been?" Tessa blew her bangs out of her eyes, a sure sign of exasperation.

"I am so sorry I'm late. I forgot that Marta Ellison was staying at my house this weekend, and she showed up right as I was getting ready to leave." This, of course, was a lie. I had still been asleep when Marta arrived. In some ways, it was fortunate she'd showed up when she did, or else I might still be sleeping.

I saw Nick and Misty working in a corner of the studio that hadn't been re-configured for the day's sessions.

Nick was working at a tabletop torch. Misty was cleaning mandrels, those thin metal rods beadmakers wrap glass around when they're making beads.

"Hey, Jax," said Misty.

"Do you need some help dipping mandrels in bead release?" I asked.

"It's okay, I'm almost done," Misty said, dunking a couple of inches of each mandrel into a jar full of what looked like a clay milkshake and then placing each wet-tipped mandrel into a hole in a wooden block to dry.

I'd chatted with Misty and Nick at Fremont Fire a few times and seen them selling their beads on the street, like yesterday. They used Tessa's studio to create batches of beads to sell. My friend supported Nick and Misty by letting them use her scrap glass, and she often gave them free rental time on the torches to help them make a few extra things to sell.

I admired some of the beads that had just come out of the cold kiln, now sitting on the counter, still on their mandrels.

"Oh, these are some of my favorites," Misty said, noticing that I was admiring her beads. "That red color—it's hard to work with."

"All right, you guys need to finish up," Tessa said. "We've got people coming in here to watch demos in about an hour."

"Yeah, we've gotta stop. No more money to keep going," Nick said, as he turned off the torch.

"Well, don't worry about paying me. You can pay me back some other time."

As Nick moved away from the torch, he knocked over a tall jar of bead release, and Misty helped him wipe up the mess on the countertop.

"I dipped some extra mandrels for you, Tessa," Misty said with a smile. She seemed happy to be able to do something nice to help Tessa in return for all she had done for them.

"Misty? How much for the red bead?" I asked.

"Is 20 dollars okay with you?"

"It's worth every cent," I said.

Misty pulled the bead off the mandrel. The bead release crumbled away as she did, leaving in its place a perfect hole. She placed the bead in my hand, delighted to have made a sale.

I handed her a bill and pocketed the bead.

"Hey, thanks," said Misty with a small wave, as she and Nick headed for the door.

"Not staying for the demos?" Tessa asked.

"Yeah, we're not really into hanging out with so many…"

"Bead ladies?"

"Uh, yeah, sort of," said Nick. And they were gone.

We bustled around, getting ready for the demos. They were scheduled to start at 11 o'clock. Just a few minutes before 11, Fremont Fire was packed with people sitting in the audience.

"Hey, Tracy," I said, noticing her taking a seat on the aisle. "I didn't think you'd make it here for the beadmaking demos."

"I've never been over here before, and it seemed like it would be fun to see some flameworking."

"Well, I'm glad you're here."

"Okay, everyone, let's get started. First up is Dylan." Tessa was trying to get everyone seated and quiet for the first demo. "He'll be making a hollow bead from borosilicate glass, also known as Pyrex." My sturdy measuring cup was made of Pyrex, and it amazed me to think that a torch could melt it.

Dylan had been hiding out in the storage room. I think he had stage fright, poor guy. Tessa coaxed him out, and he got started. As soon as Dylan lit the torch, I saw all of his nervousness melt away, and he started describing his process. He was at home behind a torch, and I smiled, watching him make a perfect pendant in front of dozens of onlookers.

I looked down and realized the chair where Tracy had been sitting was empty. How strange. Hadn't she just told me she was looking forward to seeing how beads were made? Perhaps there'd been an emergency back at the bead shop.

When Dylan finished, we all applauded for him and he took an awkward bow before he left the raised stage area.

We took a break before the next demo started. Tessa had gotten coffee sent over from Starbucks. She'd bought some donut holes and piled them high on plates on one of the side tables. By the end of the break, I had drifts of powdered sugar across my black shirt. I swear

I do not know how other people avoid looking like they were hit by a miniature blizzard when eating those little white donuts.

I brushed myself off as best I could. I'd worn a necklace, made of beads, of course, that I'd wrapped around my neck a couple of times to make a choker. I unwound it and put it back on as one long necklace, hoping to camouflage any speckles of white sugar remaining on my shirt.

Tessa took the stage once again. "Next up is Saundra Jameson. Many of you know Saundra from her popular *Bead Diva* book series. We are excited to have Saundra here to demonstrate how to make one of her animal-print beads."

This likely explained why Judy from JOWL had been wearing a large tiger-striped bead yesterday. Saundra must have made it.

The Bead Diva took the stage, looking elegant in her long flowing skirt and kimono-style jacket. Saundra tied her long hair back with a satin ribbon and removed her jacket. She donned a work tunic so she wouldn't ruin what she was wearing if a hot sliver of glass landed on her while she was working. That happens from time to time to any beadmaker. One thing that meant for me—since I didn't own a fancy work tunic—was that most of the jeans and shirts I owned had tiny burn holes in them.

"Hello, everyone. I'm glad so many people showed up to watch *me* demo today," said Saundra.

"Came specifically to see her?" I said to Tessa, as we stood at the back of the room. "Because no one would show up to see the other riff-raff?"

"Shhhhh," Tessa scolded.

"Today I'll be creating a bead I've only demonstrated on one other occasion, and that was when I was asked to show some high-value donors how to make one of my signature beads at a fundraising event," Saundra continued, sounding pleased with herself.

"Diva and saint," Tessa whispered, looking at Saundra with at least as much disdain as Saundra had for everyone else in the room. "Listen, I've got to go herd some more cats to keep these demos going."

Hearing Tessa mention cats, even if hers were metaphorical, reminded me of Gumdrop. "Tessa, you are not going to believe this, but Gumdrop has flown the coop!" I told her what happened, and filled her in on Marta and the not-very-welcome Stanley. Tessa gave me a big hug and wished for Gumdrop's safe return, and then went off to find the next performer in today's three-ring circus.

Saundra was still going strong when I finished my update with Tessa. Saundra went on. And on and on and on. "In order to make the tiger-striped bead—and remember, you can find full instructions in my book *Bead Diva 3: Jungle-Inspired Designs*—we start by making what is commonly called a twisty, which of course, is incorrect... As we all should know, the proper name of this is technique is the Italian word *latticino*. Next..."

I wandered off, figuring I'd sit down and read her book someday. But at that moment, I just couldn't stand her ego—it was taking up too much of the room.

I waved to Tessa as I headed for the door. She looked like she had her hands full, trying to herd Indigo Martin up to the front of the room to get ready for her demo. First, Tessa would need to find a giant hook to get Saundra off the stage.

NINE

"GUMMMMMDROOOOOPPPP!" I yelled coming in the back door. "Come on out, kitty-kitty-kitty!" There was no sign of Gumdrop. He was definitely not in the house, because he would have come out from his hiding place by now.

My cat had been gone all day, and I was worried about him. I put a bowl of food on the porch, with the hope that if Gumdrop was hiding somewhere nearby, he'd come out when he smelled the food. The overgrown rosemary bushes between the porch and the yard looked like a perfect hiding place, and I got down on my hands and knees to peer under the low branches. No luck. My dear Gummie wasn't there.

As I turned to get up, I saw a pair of work boots next to me. Attached to these boots were a man's legs—in fact, a whole man.

"Need some help?" the man said, offering me his hand. Oh, great. He must be one of Val's boyfriends, another in her never-ending stream of bad choices.

He was a tall, gangly guy with a pockmarked face. He didn't seem like one of her usual types, with his scraggly ponytail, enormous muttonchops, and harsh dark eyes. He wasn't the friendliest-looking guy I'd ever seen, although he did seem to have manners enough to help me up.

Val trotted out her front door. "Oh, hi Jax. This is Rudy, the painter you said was coming to give you a quote on doing your kitchen."

Ah. This explained why this scary man was here, although it didn't explain why he'd been in Val's house or why Val was carrying a pitcher of margaritas and two glasses. Perhaps she had finally taken my advice and realized that sometimes you have to look beyond someone's superficial appearance to see how terrific they are.

"Oh, right," I said, after being hoisted up by Rudy and straightening myself out. "Do you have a quote for me on the painting job?"

"Oh, yeah. Your kitchen." Val had distracted Rudy. I wondered if he'd even been in to see the kitchen. Humph. "Yeah, it's going to need a lot of work getting the peeling paint off the ceiling." Okay, he had definitely been in my kitchen.

"I'll send you a quote real soon. I left my card on your kitchen counter," Rudy said as he headed toward Val's door, a margarita with his name on it beckoning to him.

"Okay, you guys, see you later." There was no response as the door clicked shut.

Back inside, I sat at the kitchen table and stared up at the ceiling with its rippling paint that dated back at least 20 years. I hoped Rudy would give me a good deal on fixing it. Maybe I'd get the "neighbor-of-your-new-girlfriend" discount, but I doubted it.

I started up my Mac and went to Craigslist to see if any cats resembling Gumdrop were listed in the "Lost and Found" section. No gray cats had been found. I posted a "lost cat" message, giving a good description of my dear kitty, but leaving out the part about him being psychic, and also omitting that he was addicted to catnip.

Since I was on my laptop I decided to whip up a lost cat poster to tack up around the neighborhood. I started up Microsoft Word and typed up a description of Gummie, adding my phone number. I found a good picture of him and put it right in the middle of the page. Then I printed a few copies and headed out the door and down the street, tacking up the posters on telephone poles as I went.

On my way back up the street, I spotted Mr. Chu at his mailbox. He had an enormous orange tabby cat slung over one arm. His ratty robe was not all the way closed, revealing a dingy white T-shirt and boxer shorts.

I've met a few crazy cat ladies, but Mr. Chu was the first crazy cat man I'd ever met.

Mr. Chu was heading back down the driveway between our houses, and I caught up with him.

"Mr. Chu, hi, how are you?"

"Fine, fine," he said, holding his cat close and petting him in long strokes. Mr. Chu was a man of few words. I think he preferred cats to people.

"I'm wondering if you've seen my cat," I said, as I followed him down the driveway. "He's big and gray with long hair, and he has a bit of an attitude."

"No. Can't say I have." We'd reached Mr. Chu's back door. When he opened it, I could see a handful of cats standing inside, looking up expectantly at their owner.

"Can't let any cats out," Mr. Chu said, squeezing in the door, waving, and shutting it quickly.

My search for Gumdrop would have to continue later.

What I needed to do now was to put together a packet of instructions for the workshop I was giving on Sunday. I had a tutorial for a bracelet, using five oval white heart beads. Each bead would be wrapped with wire to create a link in a chain, then the links would be attached together to make a pretty bracelet. More components could be added using the same technique to create an entire necklace, like the one I'd brought to display at Aztec Beads for the weekend.

•   •   •

Beadmaking was a different kind of job than I'd once had. These days, it seemed like I was constantly working: making beads, designing jewelry, creating inventories, working on my website, contacting galleries, at all times of the day and night. When I worked for Clorox, it was a regular 9 to 5 job. I had job security and a consistent paycheck. I had all of that...until Aunt Rita and I decided it was time to start on my next adventure.

The day after I received the lawyer's letter, I simply went into my boss' office and said, "Terry, I'm resigning. I need a change."

"I figured you wouldn't be around much longer. You've been miserable for a while," Terry said, staring at his computer screen, not turning around.

"I'm moving to Seattle. It's a long story. It would be great if I could get out of here sooner rather than later. Any chance we can skip the two weeks' notice?"

"No problem, Jax, no problem at all." The blue glow of the computer screen illuminated his dark face. "We'll send you a final check. Make sure you leave us your new address."

"Thanks so much, Terry, you're changing my life." I said, trying to work up some enthusiasm in him.

"No problem. Have a nice life," he said, as he continued to review his latest test results.

That. Was. It. Not even a handshake goodbye. I walked down the white hall, through the white door, and into a world of living color.

• • •

A knock on the back door jolted me out of my reverie. I fully expected it would be Marta, there to show me what a good job Stanley had done making a piddle, or a pee-pee, or whatever.

"Dylan," I said with surprise, as I opened the door. "What are you doing here?"

"I'm just nervous about going to the party tonight. You know, it's all a bunch of bead ladies, and then *me*."

"What, you want me to make you an honorary bead lady? It can be done, you know," I said with mock seriousness.

"It's just that I don't fit in, you know?" Dylan said, looking down at the table, dejected. He noticed the stack of class instructions. "You ready to teach your class?"

"I am. I think I am. Maybe," I said, shuffling through the papers to make sure they were all complete.

"I dunno, Jax, maybe I should give it up. I mean, nobody takes me seriously." "Look, Dylan: I take you seriously. Tessa takes you seriously. You take yourself seriously, right? That's enough. Go home, put on some nice clothes," I said, eyeing his old T-shirt, holey jeans and flip-flops, "and get ready to schmooze some people tonight. Maybe you'll meet a jewelry designer who wants to place a huge order for your excellent beads."

Dylan stood there, staring down at his saggy pants. "I can't really afford any new clothes. The new apartment is pretty much wiping my bank account clean each month."

"Well, we can't have that, can we?" I said, grabbing my handbag. "Uh…"

"Come on, Dylan, nobody is going to take you seriously unless you up your game, okay? So, let's get moving. I'm going to be your fairy godmother."

"Fairy god—"

"That's right Dylan. Fairy. God. Mother. You know, she gets Cinderella a new dress to go to the ball." I turned and opened the studio door, and gestured toward the Ladybug.

"Sire, your carriage awaits."

Dylan looked at me uncertainly. "Let's go," I said, trying to clear up the picture for him. "I'm going to buy you an outfit to wear tonight." This had not been part of the plan for my busy day, but I've always been a sucker for a good cause.

"I won't buy you anything crazy, or anything that's going to make you feel uncomfortable. Just something nice." Val's love of makeovers was apparently contagious. "I'm not going to spend a lot; we're just going to get you something that will make you feel confident, and maybe that confidence will mean someone wants to buy a few extra beads."

"Just the two of us?" Dylan asked timidly, as I opened the car door and pushed him in. I came around to the driver's side and swung myself into the seat.

I gave him a sideways glance. "Why?"

"Well, I think your neighbor, Val, dresses nice. Maybe she could come?"

My head came to rest on the steering wheel. Val. If I invited her to come on this little makeover adventure, I would never hear the end of it.

"Sure, Dylan, if that would make you happy," I sighed. "Let's go talk with Val and see if she can come." I hoped Rudy had already left, or that Val would simply not open the door if we were interrupting something.

We got back out of the car and came around the side of the house, narrowly missing a pile of poop Stanley had left behind. Dammit, Marta, get your shit together. Literally. Figuratively.

Dylan followed after me like my own puppy. When we arrived at Val's door a few seconds later, we knocked and Val opened the door.

"Yessssss?" she said, with a curious smile.

"Dylan and I were wondering if you'd like to go shopping with us," I said, subtly craning my neck around Val to see if Rudy was inside.

"Becaussssssse…" she prompted me to continue, leaning saucily against the doorjamb.

I took a deep breath. "Because Dylan here needs a new outfit to wear for the party tonight, and so I said I'd buy him something."

"But really, Jax, you don't—" said Dylan.

"I want to—"

"People! People!" Val said, clapping her hands to get our attention.

We both stopped and looked at her, our mouths still open but no words coming out.

"You know that expression, you should 'shop your closet' when you don't have anything to wear?" Val asked.

"No," Dylan and I said in unison.

Val sighed. "Well, the idea is that before you buy anything new, you should make sure you don't already have the perfect thing hiding in your closet. But there is another saying, a corollary."

"Corollary?" we said in unison.

"Yes, corollary!" Val said. I have to admit that while I knew what a corollary was, I was surprised Val did. "The corollary is: When you can't find anything in your own closet, shop your neighbor's closet."

I had never seen Val so pumped up. "Don't you worry, Dylan, I will take care of you."

Dylan looked nervous. I'm sure he was regretting his idea of asking Val along on our shopping spree. We were both assessing our options for a getaway plan.

Val grabbed both of us by the wrists, and yanked us inside. It was too late to escape now. She'd closed us in, and we were trapped in her living room with her animal print pillows and bright pink sofa.

"I have a few things here that might work, and it might mean Jax can save her hard-earned money." Val was talking a mile a minute.

"You see," she said, by way of explanation, "I've had a few boyfriends."

"Just a few," I agreed, being more than a little snarky.

"And sometimes they leave things behind. I have here a giant box of men's clothing," Val said, returning from her bedroom and struggling to see over the top of the box she carried.

"I'm getting clothing worn by a bunch of old dudes?" asked Dylan.

"*Not* old," said Val. "I do not date old guys."

"Val, your donation to Dylan's cause is very generous," I said, "but…" I knew this wasn't going to work out. Her heart was in the right place, but a bunch of questionable clothing from some guys who were also pretty questionable seemed like a less-than-perfect situation.

"Look, I'm just trying to help here, and save you some money—"

"I know, Val, but geez, Dylan's not going to like, or fit into, any of these clothes. I mean—"

"You always think the guys I date are losers. I don't—"

"Hey, check it out," Dylan said, beaming and mock modeling for us, turning side to side to show us how excellent he looked. While we'd been arguing, Dylan had picked out a shirt from the box and pulled it over his ratty T-shirt.

He was wearing a simple gray long-sleeved dress shirt and was on his way to looking fabulous. Dylan was such a sweet man, still just a boy, really.

"Here's a belt," said Val, starting to stuff it through his belt loops. "This will help make those saggy pants look better."

"You have any shoes in there?" I asked.

"I'm afraid I don't," said Val. "Guys seem to leave shirts behind much more often than shoes."

"Actually…I've got just the solution for the shoes," I said. "I'll be right back."

I ran out Val's door and then back into my front door, nearly colliding with Marta, who had returned from Tessa's studio, and Stanley.

"We're going for a run," Marta said.

Poor Stanley didn't look like he was up for a run. Marta noticed Stanley was looking droopier than usual. "Maybe we'll just go for a walk today."

I came back to Val's five minutes later with a pair of black sneakers.

"Look at these shoes. These would work, right?"

"Well…" said Val, examining them as if they were something dead I'd scraped off the road.

"Come on, these are exactly what you need," I told Dylan. "They're black, and they are sort of unisex, right?"

"Well…" said Dylan.

"Seriously, Dylan? You're going to turn up your nose at these perfectly good shoes? I'm pretty sure they'll fit you; they've always been too big for me. Better than flip-flops, right?"

"See, I kind of have my own shoes, I just don't ever wear them. I like flip-flops better. They just feel more natural. They let my feet breathe, ya know?"

"Okay, so, what you're saying is that you already have good shoes. Why didn't you just say so?"

Val gently folded the shirt, brushing out its wrinkles, and placed it in a fancy shopping bag along with Dylan's new belt.

"Go home now, and I'll see you looking faboo at the party tonight," called Val as Dylan headed for the door, making his escape before she tried any more makeover moves on him. I'd personally make sure Val, a hairdresser, never cut Dylan's shaggy blond hair. It was perfect for him.

"Thanks, ladies. Later." Dylan took his new shirt and belt with him, and we watched as he loped down the street.

"Well, I've got to get going. You know I need at least an hour to get this," Val gestured Vanna White-style to her curvaceous body, "ready to par-tay!"

"You go get all of *that* ready," I said, gesturing wildly at her, "and I'll go take care of *this*," I continued, gesturing this time, pathetically, at my own untucked T-shirt, jeans, and sneakers I'd thrown on this morning. At least I had a terrific necklace to camouflage the dozen or so white specks from the donut holes I'd eaten earlier.

As I headed out the door, I could hear Val yell, "Don't forget to wear something nice and prett—" I shut the door quickly, before she finished giving me her advice.

I was relieved I didn't have to do the fairy godmother thing after all, because now I had more time to get ready for my workshop—and more time to try to put myself together for the party.

TEN

ON THE RARE OCCASION when I need to dress up, my standard party attire is black from head to toe, or at least from cleavage to knee. But today, for some reason, I couldn't get behind that fashion choice. Instead, I went with red. Full on, fire engine red. I knew that I was never going to be this young again. In fact, I was getting older every second, so I might as well be bold. At least for one night.

I had a cute dress I'd never had the guts to wear, but I thought I'd finally whip it out for tonight's party. The dress was a wraparound style, and it was great, because it could expand or contract based on my current size. Val had been making some delicious desserts recently, and even some of the failed ones were amazing. I was grateful the dress had this valuable feature, given my recently expanded size. Val, as might have been expected, had helped me pick this dress, and while she was comfortable flaunting her own voluptuous features, I must admit I wasn't comfortable looking this curvy in public.

I pulled on my trusty Spanx to hold all the curves in the right places, jumping up and down and holding the waistband to squeeze myself into them.

Then I put on the biggest red necklace I'd ever made. Each of the 11 spherical beads in the necklace had a red core and a layer of gold leaf. On top of the gold was a thick layer of crystal clear glass, and tiny flowers and vines swirled around the outside of each bead. Between each of the larger orbs was a small gold disk that coordinated with the gold leaf deep inside each bead.

I knew it was important to wear a fantastic necklace tonight. There'd be designers and wholesale buyers at Rosie's reception. I hoped, by wearing this fabulous necklace to show off my work, someone might want to place an order right there on the spot. If the price were right, I'd sell this necklace right off my body. I could always make another one. I put on a matching bracelet and the tallest black pumps I owned—which weren't really that tall because I'm a wimp when it comes to high heels.

I fluffed up my short hair. I'd always worn my hair past my shoulders, but these days I was wearing it in a pixie-cut following an unfortunate incident earlier this year when I'd leaned inside a hot kiln and singed my bangs. On a good hair day, I looked like Tinker Bell. On a bad hair day, I looked like Billy Idol. Fortunately, today was a Tinker Bell day.

My light brown hair was getting blonder by the year, because every time the gray hairs started overtaking the brown ones, I went to Val's salon and had her eradicate them with a few highlights. She always pleaded with me to let her do something new to my hair—low-lights or a Brazilian blowout. And lately she'd been going on and on about ombre, whatever that meant. I always resisted.

I swept some bronzer across my cheeks. Since I'd moved to Seattle, I missed having a little tan on my face. Thanks to my Irish genes, I usually burned and freckled, but I did like the rosy glow I could get from being out in the sun each day. I added a swipe of mascara and some tinted lip balm, and I was ready to go. I knew Val would be disappointed I didn't go full-throttle with glitter eye shadow and burgundy lips, but I had become pretty low-maintenance during the last few years, and I could never pull off the over-the-top sparkly makeup Val wore so well.

I took a look in the mirror. Not too bad.

I was feeling good and looking forward to the party. I felt like I could use some fun, especially after last night's fiasco with Allen.

Ugh. Allen. I wondered if he'd be at the party tonight. According to Tessa, Judy had invited him to all of the weekend's events. I figured he'd never want to see me again. I was embarrassed, and hoped I never saw him again. Ever.

Marta came home all red-cheeked and sweaty. Poor Stanley was panting heavily. He galloped into the kitchen, as best as he could with his stumpy five-inch legs, found Gumdrop's water bowl, and slurped down every drop in it. Then he stood there, water dripping down each fold on his furry face, and looked at me expectantly with his pathetic bloodshot eyes. I picked up the bowl, filled it, and set it down. He drank it.

Oh, the poor guy was so thirsty.

I picked up the bowl and filled it again. And he emptied it again. Marta finally came into the kitchen.

"Is it okay he's having all this water?" I asked Marta.

"Oh, as long as it's only one bowl, he's fine. If he has much more than that, he tends to have accidents."

"This is at least his third, possibly fourth, bowl," I said, trying to sound calm but feeling like yelling. Okay, actually, I may have been yelling.

"Oh, gosh! Well, we'll just have to be extra careful. Won't we, my widdle cutie pie? We don't want any oopsies," said Marta. I was fairly certain she was now talking with Stanley, and not me. I swear, this woman was going to kill me with her baby talk.

"Right. Well, there are spare paper towels under the sink, in case you need them to clean up any 'oopsies.'"

The doorbell rang and I ran to answer it, but Val burst through the door without waiting. She looked me up and down. I stood at attention as she inspected me.

"Hmmmm. Red. Very fiery. I like it. Faboo necklace. Oh, and a matching bracelet, that's a nice touch," Val said as she circled me. "You pass."

I exhaled, glad she considered me acceptable to be seen in public. Val had on enough glitter for both of us, and she had her hair piled up on her head, which added a good four inches to her height. The high heels added another four inches. With the heels and hair, Val was well over six feet tall. She made me feel downright petite at only five-and-a-half feet.

"Ready?" Val asked me, adjusting her cleavage in the mirror by the front door.

"Let me go and get my handbag."

I rushed down the hall, and as I turned the corner into my bedroom, I skidded across something wet on the floor. I crashed into the wall, knocking a painting of a tropical sunset of its hook. I caught it before it hit the ground, thanks to my fast reflexes, and gently hung it back up.

"Are you okay back there?" Val asked.

"Oh fine, there's a piddle, I mean *puddle*, on the floor," I said, looking down at my shoes, which were wet around the edges. Stanley was the worst houseguest ever, and Marta was high up on the list as well.

I returned a few minutes later, having changed shoes, and was frankly wearing much more reasonable ones now. I'd taken off the high heels and put on my trusty Mary Janes.

Val was standing at the front door, checking her backside in the mirror. "My car?"

"That'd be great," I said.

"That way when the sexy guy who was over last night shows up at the party, he can give you a ride home," Val said, pursing her lips and raising one eyebrow.

"How do you know about Allen?"

"I see all, remember? I live, like, 12 inches from you. I saw him arrive, and I saw him leave a few hours later."

"Snoop!"

"At one point I heard some screaming, but I wasn't sure if that was a good thing."

"Eavesdropper!" I said, "Also, it wasn't a good thing."

"He was walking strangely when he left…"

"I don't want to talk about it."

ELEVEN

IT HAD BEEN RAINING earlier in the afternoon, but fortunately it had stopped. I was glad the party could spill outside onto the patio behind Aztec Beads, so we wouldn't all be crushed inside during the reception.

As we arrived, we saw Misty and Nick standing on the sidewalk, loading jewelry into their backpacks. Misty saw me and gave a little wave, but she kept packing. She seemed to be in a hurry, so Val and I went into the shop.

The air in Aztec Beads felt brittle with tension. Rosie was alone at the front window, looking out as Misty and Nick finished gathering their things and headed down the street past the gallery window. Rosie's body was nearly vibrating with anger.

I approached Rosie cautiously, hoping that, unlike Tito, she wouldn't try to bite me.

"Hi, Rosie," I said, trying to get her to shift her attention away from the window. I looked out toward the gallery and the patio. Several people had already arrived and were mingling. "Looks like some people are already here," I said, stating the obvious. Rosie continued to stare out the window, hands on hips. Her face, reflected in the window, was smug, as if she had personally booted

Misty and Nick off the sidewalk, when they probably just left on their own.

"Rosie?"

"Oh, Jax," Rosie said, finally unlocking her glare. "Glad you could make it."

She was wearing a denim skirt with a sash tied around her waist and a silky white blouse. It was the perfect outfit for showing off a special piece of jewelry.

"Wow, Rosie," I gushed, "that is a *fantastic* necklace." It was a long strand of impressive artisan-made glass beads, each a couple of inches long. There were all sorts of shapes and styles: sculptural animals, vessels, polka-dotted beads, disks, and elongated barrel shapes, separated by segments of pea-sized silver beads so that each handmade bead stood apart from the others. The necklace was long, and since Rosie was on the short side, she'd artfully wrapped it around her neck a couple of times.

"Where did you get such a terrific necklace?" I asked.

"Oh, it's my very special collection, beads from 20 different bead-makers. I've collected them over the past several years. They mean so much to me; I've got a story to tell about each one."

"Well, you wear it well," I said, picking up the necklace from Rosie's chest and admiring several of the beads more closely. "Oh, and here's one Tessa made."

"That's one of my favorites." Rosie seemed to have forgotten her anger about Misty and Nick, and I was thankful for that. I'm sure she wanted tonight's party to be a success. Even if she wasn't in the mood, it was in her best interest to put on a happy face.

"Rosie, this is my friend Val."

"Hi, Val, what kind of beads do you make?"

"I actually don't make beads."

"Oh, then you design necklaces?"

"No, actually I —"

"Wholesale buyer?"

"No, I just—"

"Well, nice to meet you." Rosie turned and abruptly departed.

Val and I looked at each other. "What was that about?" Val asked.

"I have no idea, but I don't think people skills are Rosie's strong suit," I replied. "I guess she figures if you're coming to this event, you're into beads. And if you're not into beads, then she has no use for you."

"Well, I do like beads. I don't have to make them to love them, right?"

"Right. Kind of like kids. I don't need to have one of my own to love Tessa's kids."

"I'll drink to that," said Val, who could frankly drink to just about anything.

Rosie had strung some strands of tiny lights around the patio, added some outdoor heaters to help keep everyone warm outside in the chilly Seattle night, and set up tables for food and drinks. Someone had hooked up an iPod to a set of huge speakers that were blasting fun dance music, although there may have been some artistic differences about what type of music to play. The soundtrack was alternating between Latin rhythms and '80s pop.

Marta showed up at the party right after we did and tracked me down like a hound.

"Jax, sorry, but you didn't give me a key to your house. I couldn't lock the front door. I left Stanley there, and I've got to get back to him."

"I'll get a spare key for you. But the good news is Stanley can guard the house in the meantime," I said.

"I'm worried someone might break in and steal him."

"Steal him?" I couldn't believe anyone would want him, let alone break into my house to take him.

"He's a valuable dog," Marta said.

Knowing I wouldn't be able to convince her that Stanley would be perfectly safe at my house without locking up, I went in search of Val. I found her by the front door, trying to convince Judy from JOWL that a new haircut would change her life. And, of course, that Val was just the right person to give her that new style.

I sidled up to Val. "Give me the spare key to my house. Do you still have it?"

"What? Are you taking away my key privileges?" Val responded. "Does this mean I'm going to have to start breaking in again?"

"What do you mean 'again'?" I asked, wondering just how much time Val spent at my place when I wasn't home.

"Oh, nothing, nothing," Val said. She started rummaging through her giant silver shoulder bag and pulling out things to loosen up all of the junk in there. A brush, a cell phone covered with rhinestones, Tic-Tacs, another brush, mirror, lip-gloss, lipstick, lip-liner, lip-plumper...

"Val, how many lip products does a woman need?"

"Oh, about this many when I'm out and about, but I've got more in the car for backup."

She pulled out a small pair of pliers. Pliers? What in the world did she need with a pair of pliers? Address book, nail file, scissors, and finally, a set of keys.

"Here you go," Val said, removing the key from her miniature disco ball key ring and pressing it into my hand. "When do I get it back?" She looked at me with a pout.

"When Marta leaves on Monday. Let me give this key to her, and I'll be right back."

I dashed back to Marta and gave her the key. "You'll go right now and lock up?"

"Of course. I've got to keep my widdle puppy-wuppy safe. See you back here in a little while," she said with a wide toothy grin.

"Okay." I had absolutely nothing to say to her about her "widdle puppy," other than I wished she'd left her annoying dog at home in Idaho.

"We are going have so much fun tonight when we get back to your house—it will be like a slumber party," Marta said.

"Uh, yes. A slumber party," I said, trying to match her enthusiasm, and failing. I remembered what slumber parties were like when I was growing up: staying up all night, too much junk food, someone throwing up, and usually someone in tears.

"Looking forward to that," I said, mustering a weak smile as Marta, her stubby ponytail bouncing, headed out the door.

TWELVE

AS WE LOOKED AT the jewelry on each pedestal, I told Val about the artists in the exhibition.

"This is the work of Indigo Martin," I said, as we approached one of the pedestals. We were looking at a necklace of sculpted leaf beads in a gorgeous palette of autumn colors: red, orange, russet, and an earthy brown. There were delicate tendrils of tiny beads wrapped around the glass leaves to complete the necklace. Indigo was a beautiful black woman who was well known for her nature-inspired jewelry and notorious for her flaky behavior. I looked around the room, but I didn't see her in the crowd.

"Indigo thinks she's still living in the '60s, all peace signs and daisies. She's coming to the reception; I'll introduce you."

"Yuck! I'm not sure if I'll like someone who wears peasant shirts and bell bottoms," said Val, looking disgusted.

"Well, why don't you hold off judging someone until you meet her?"

"Pffft!" Val gave me a lady-like raspberry. "I'm going to find the snacks."

"Very mature," I said, as she sashayed away.

I ran into The Twins next. They were not actual twins, but rather two women who had chosen to look nearly identical in their long black dresses, pale skin, and blood-red lips. They'd had this Goth look for as long as I'd known them, and their jewelry reflected their funereal fashion sense. Around each of their necks hung beautiful rosary-type necklaces full of crosses, skulls, pentacles, and ankhs. They were definitely covering all their bases in terms of mystical and religious icons. Their beads were gorgeous in their black, purple, and ruby palette.

Sara and Lara were known as Dark Star Beads. It was a cosmic coincidence that their names rhymed, they assured me. Each young woman was equally talented, and they were absolutely impossible to tell apart. Whenever I thought I'd figured it out, something would change. For a while, Sara had a birthmark on her cheek, making it easy to know who was who. One day, her birthmark was gone, having migrated to the area below the corner of Lara's mouth. Apparently this birthmark was applied with black eyeliner and could disappear with just a dab of makeup remover.

"Jax," The Twins said simultaneously. This was their version of a warm greeting.

"Hi there," I said, being clever and avoiding calling them by their individual names. "How are you?"

"Awful," said one.

"Terrible," said the other.

"Why? What's up?"

"Oh, we hate events like this," said Sara, or possibly Lara.

"Yes, we always have to be cheerful at receptions when meeting potential clients," said the other one, scowling. They were clearly not clued in to what it meant to be cheerful.

"And no one seems to understand our work," the first one continued. "People who view our work—they've got to understand the existentialism in our work, the dark zeitgeist, the impossibility of redemption."

I was certain I didn't understand what her beads "meant," and I'm not sure she did, either. Their beads were dark, and some were almost scary. But, in that darkness, there was unusual beauty, and that's what mattered most to me.

"I think they're pretty," I said, not knowing how else to respond to the multi-syllabic gobbledygook, that Lara—or Sara—had just spouted.

"Whatever," they said together, and walked off, their long, straight, blue-black hair swaying in unison as they left.

"So, those are The Twins," I said to Val, when I turned and found her at the appetizer table on the patio a few feet away.

"And do you call them that to their face?" asked Val.

"Oh, no, they wouldn't be amused." In fact, I didn't think they'd be amused by much of anything.

"They have that Goth look. Is that still a 'thing'?" Val asked, more as a criticism than a question.

"Yes, it's still a 'thing.'"

"Well, it seems so passé. Everyone was doing the Goth thing in the '90s. I mean, even *I* did the Goth thing back then. I'll have to show you pictures some time."

Now *that* I had to see. Val was the most non-Goth (un-Goth?) person in the world.

"Seriously," Val continued, "I had this one black corset—"

"Val, get a grip. I don't want to hear about your underwear."

"Underwear? Oh no, honey, you don't understand, I wore this corset on the outside, I—" Val continued as she picked up a cube of cheese with her long fingernails.

"Yuck! Val! Use a toothpick to pick up the cheese."

"Who died and made you Miss Manners?" Val asked rhetorically, as she popped the cheese in her mouth.

I saw Dylan sneak in the garden's back gate. He looked overwhelmed to see so many people. I squeezed through a group gathered at the wine table, filling their plastic glasses with what I hoped wasn't terrible chardonnay, since I planned to have a glass.

"Dylan, you look terrific. I've never seen you look so...so...suave." Dylan looked at me, perplexed.

"You know, handsome, well-put-together, fashionable and cool, all mixed together."

"Yeah, Jax, I know what suave means," Dylan said, looking more serious than I'd ever seen him before.

"Why are you coming in the back way?"

"I don't like big groups, ya know? I was hoping I could just kinda come in quietly and check out the scene, under the radar."

"Well, don't worry, stick with me," I said, trying to reassure him.

Spotting Dylan, Val charged toward us like a giant glittering rhino. Val wouldn't be amused by my simile. I would need to keep it to myself, or face being stomped on by one of her rhino-sized stilettos.

"Oh my," said Val. I swear she was tearing up. "Oh, I…" She was speechless, an unusual state for Val. She grabbed Dylan in the biggest hug I'd ever seen. Dylan looked tiny compared to Val, as she gripped him in a full-body hug. He hung there, arms loose, looking like a ragdoll in Val's arms. Fortunately, she released him before he passed out. If Dylan wasn't overwhelmed before, he was now.

"Hey, Val. How's it goin'?" Dylan asked, trying to regain some composure and straighten out his new (slightly used) clothes.

"Dylan, you must show me your beads," said Val, trying to move on from what was too dramatic a moment even for her. Val took Dylan's arm, locked it into hers, and dragged him away. Poor Dylan. I hoped he'd survive the night.

I felt a tap on my shoulder and turned around to see a chubby man standing beside me. "Are you Jax?"

"Yes, I am," I said, because, really, I couldn't deny it.

"Oh, Jax, I am soooo glad to meet you. I saw your work in the gallery. I'm Frankie Lawton," the man said, extending his hand to shake, like Stanley-the-dog, palm down.

I wasn't sure if I should shake his hand or kiss his ring. I gave his hand a tentative squeeze, as I had done with Stanley.

Frankie was a jewelry designer who had recently become a superstar in the world of high fashion. The model on the cover of last month's *Vogue* magazine was wearing one of his necklaces and a pair of earrings, and that meant the demand for Frankie's work had skyrocketed. Frankie was wearing a red jacket and pants, a white shirt, and wide black belt. All he needed was a white beard and a red hat, and he'd look like Santa. A stylish, gay Santa.

"Oh, wow, Frankie, I am extremely pleased to meet you," I said, in what was probably too enthusiastic a manner.

"Your work is stupendous! Stupendous!" Frankie said.

"Thank you. You have no idea how much this means to me..." I stopped just short of gushing and embarrassing myself.

I saw Tito run by, carrying a cracker he'd clearly found under the appetizer table. When he was finished with his snack, he ran over to us and looked up expectantly. I assumed he was hoping we'd give him something else to eat. I tried to ignore him, but kept a cautious eye on him, since I knew he'd rather bite than bark. Suddenly Tito lunged at the cuff on Frankie's red trousers, pulling and shaking his head from side to side.

"I don't know why Rosie doesn't keep Tito under house arrest," Frankie said.

"Shoo! Shoo!" I yelled at the dog, waving my hands around, but not too close, trying to get him to let go of Frankie's pants.

Just as quickly as he had attacked, Tito let go and ran off to abuse another guest at the party.

Frankie regained his composure and looked down to see if the dog had done any damage to his cuff. From what I could tell, it looked fine, and we were able to continue our conversation.

"I'm interested in purchasing some of the beads you have on display in the shop. But right now, I *must* run off to my next event. I'll find you this weekend, so we can have a tête-à-tête. Okay?"

I was ecstatic. A famous designer wanted to work with me. If Frankie used my beads in a new jewelry line, I would finally make some money with my new career in glass and could stop dipping into Aunt Rita's savings account.

Feeling nearly delirious from the good news, I wandered through the crowd and back inside. Rosie came by while I was standing by my display. Amazingly, she didn't notice the pedestal looked exactly as it had the day before. Perhaps one of the reasons Rosie hadn't noticed (other than the fact that it didn't look that bad in the first place) was the subtle way I was standing in front of it, blocking her view.

I called Dylan over. I wanted him to meet Rosie, hoping that if she got to know him she might sell some of his beads in the store after the weekend's events had ended.

"Rosie, have you met Dylan?"

Dylan turned around to face Rosie. Both faces froze as they stared at each other. Between Dylan's shyness and Rosie's lack of people skills, it looked like they'd stand there forever. How did Rosie expect to run a business when she couldn't even hold out her hand and say hello? Fortunately, Tessa found me and rescued me from the awkward moment by grabbing my hand and dragging me out to the patio.

"Our favorite song!" she said, squeezing through the crowd and onto the grass so we could dance. As we were bopping around with a dozen other people to "Rock Lobster" by the B-52's, I saw Allen standing on the patio with a glass of wine. He was watching us dance.

"Who's the guy over there checking you out?" Tessa shouted over the music.

I glanced over. "Allen Sinclair."

"Wow. I had no idea I'd set you up with such a cutie. I should have had him interview *me*."

"You're married, so the fact that he's a cutie probably doesn't—or at least shouldn't—matter to you."

"Rock Lobster!" we shouted as the song ended. There was a momentary silence as we left the dance floor, or more accurately, "dance lawn," which was shredded.

"Wow, Jax, good thing that song is only four minutes long. I'm not sure I could've kept dancing much longer," Tessa said, patting her forehead with the back of her hand. Her curiosity was killing her, I could tell. "Did things go well with Allen last night? I mean really, really well?"

I was doubled-over with a stitch in my side from dancing. I definitely needed to get out of the studio more often for aerobic activity. "What? You think I'm going to kiss and tell?"

"Yes, I suppose so. Especially since I set you up with him. You owe me."

"I owe you?" I said, finally uncurling myself and looking straight at Tessa. "Well, in that case. The whole thing was a disaster, Tessa. Outrageously awful! Ridiculously terrible! Unbelievably bad!" My voice went up an octave with each new adjective.

I described in gory detail Gumdrop's high-dive into Allen's drink and the abrupt end to our evening.

As the volume and pitch of my voice increased, Tessa squeezed her eyes closed tighter and tighter, grimacing with each escalation in my tone.

We heard a crash and a scream from somewhere near the front door and dashed inside to see what had happened.

THIRTEEN

WE FOUND TRACY behind the counter, cleaning up red wine and a broken wineglass from the floor. The beautiful new carpet was now stained ruby red, and Tracy was trying frantically to clean it up.

Rosie stood over Tracy, berating her. "You stupid, stupid girl!" shouted Rosie. "I don't know why I put up with you, why I've supported you all these years."

"Stop it, Mama! It was an accident."

"Well, your life's been one big accident, hasn't it, Tracy? When are you going to grow up and take some responsibility?"

"It was a glass of wine! It's not the end of the world!"

"Do *not* argue with me in front of customers!"

"No, Mama, I've got to be the 'good girl' all the time, right?"

Suddenly, Rosie noticed an entire room of partygoers was staring at her and her daughter.

"Excuse me. I need to freshen up," Rosie said to a few of us standing close by, without making eye contact. She hurried up the inside staircase into her apartment.

"Here, Tracy, let me help you," I said. "Look, here's some soda water." I grabbed a bottle from the nearby makeshift bar. "It may have some lemon in it, but it's supposed to be good at taking out stains." I took a pile of napkins off the table, too, and started to soak up the liquid. I mopped up as much wine as I could. Tracy could clean up the mess more thoroughly once the guests departed.

I was down on my knees in my too-tight dress, wondering how I was going to get back up without showing everyone the Spanx and everything else up my dress. A hand, palm up, appeared next to my shoulder.

"May I help you up, miss?" said Allen.

"Absolutely," I said, taking his hand and hoisting myself up as gracefully as possible. As I straightened up, I saw Tracy bolt out the back door.

"Hi, Allen. How are you? Recovered from Gumdrop's acrobatics?" I asked, trying to make light of what was possibly the most embarrassing experience in my life. Actually, I've had many embarrassing experiences, but this one was at least in the top ten.

"Oh, yes. I'm resilient, although my cords need some serious washing, and I may never be able to drink another mojito. Don't worry, I'm fine. Just fine," he assured me, with a brilliant smile.

Oh, good. That made one of us.

Judy ascended a few steps of the staircase by the front counter to make some announcements.

"Hello!" she shouted, trying to get everyone's attention. "Hello!" Judy tried again. No one was paying attention or quieting down.

Marta got up on the step next to Judy. She stuck her fingers in her mouth and let rip a piercing whistle. It was impressive and effective. The room fell silent. "I am overwhelmed and overjoyed to see everyone here for our first-ever Weekend of Education, Enlightenment and Design!" Judy said.

"WEED!" I whispered in Allen's ear. He stifled a laugh.

"We've got some super workshops lined up for you tomorrow and Sunday. If you've not already done so, I hope you'll sign up for a class. I'll be around all weekend. If you need anything, I'm here for you. Everyone, please enjoy this evening, and a huge round of applause to Rosie for hosting this party, and to all the artists who are here this weekend to share their lovely beads and jewelry designs."

Dylan slid up next to me on the side opposite Allen. "Jax, can we talk later?" he asked quietly, so he wouldn't interrupt Judy's announcements.

"Sure, Dylan," I replied, still listening to Judy.

Judy finished her speech and we all applauded. I looked around to see if Rosie had come back down to hear our appreciative clapping. I couldn't see her anywhere and suspected she was up in the apartment, trying to calm down.

"Now, how about a drink? One *without* mint or catnip?" I asked Allen.

"An excellent idea." He took my hand and led me through the crowd and toward the front door.

"Wait a minute, there are drinks right next to us."

"Ah, but it's so noisy, so many people."

"I know, but listen, I can't leave the party. I'm here to support Rosie. And Tessa is in there somewhere. And Dylan, he wanted to talk with me. I—"

"Okay, okay," Allen said.

"But I have a great idea. You go get a couple of chairs and bring them out front." There was no way I was going to be able to sit on the curb in this dress, and if I did, I doubted I'd ever be able to get back up again, without a team of professional body-builders doing some heavy lifting of my backside. "I'll get some wine and glasses and meet you out there in five minutes. We'll make our own sidewalk café."

Before Allen could respond, I was gone, dashing to the make-shift bar. The ice bucket was empty—only a few inches of water remained. Tucked at the back of the buffet was a lone bottle of chardonnay that I nabbed. It was warm. Ugh! Warm white wine was the worst. Desperate times called for desperate measures, so I grabbed the empty ice bucket. I caught Allen's eye as he headed out the door with the chairs, and pantomimed that I was going upstairs to get ice. There'd be a refrigerator in Rosie's kitchen, and I hoped I'd find some ice to chill the wine.

I dashed up the inside staircase behind the front counter to the apartment and found the kitchen near the landing. I opened the freezer, grabbed the ice tray and, as I started knocking the cubes into the bucket, I heard screaming, this time from right outside on the balcony. It sounded like Tracy again. I hoped she hadn't spilled a bowl of guacamole this time, because Rosie would explode if Tracy ruined the carpet *and* a perfectly good avocado as well.

I dropped the ice bucket and dashed out of the kitchen, rounding the corner into the small living room. Tracy was on her knees on the balcony outside, crying and calling for help. Her mother had fallen on the stairs leading down to the garden. Tracy was frantically trying to pick her up. Since Rosie outweighed her daughter by at least 50 pounds, Tracy's attempts to pull her mom up the stairs were futile.

"Let me help!" I yelled, running through the open sliding glass door toward them. Rosie was lying face-up, her body sliding down the stairs. She'd been thrashing a moment before, but now she wasn't moving.

"Rosie! Rosie!" She didn't respond when I called her name. I tried to roll her over to see if a different position might help her, but she didn't budge. Then I saw it: a loop of beads twisted around the scrollwork on the balcony's railing. The necklace ran down and around Rosie's neck, and then came back up and connected to the beads on the balcony.

Rosie's necklace was strangling her!

I tried to pull it loose, but Rosie was sliding down the stairs, and the cord around her neck pulled tighter and tighter. Tracy was crying, and trying to help, but she just didn't have the strength to move her mom.

"We've got to cut this wire on the necklace," I shouted, hoping someone would hear me. Since the music on the patio below us was loud, no one could hear anything up on the balcony.

"Hey, I thought I'd come up and help you with the ice," Allen said as he rounded the corner into the living room, but he stopped in his tracks when he came upon our frantic rescue scene on the balcony.

"Quick, Allen, what can you find that will cut wire?"

"A kitchen knife!" He ran to the kitchen, grabbed a knife, and was back in seconds.

"Cut right here," I said, pointing to a spot on the necklace above Rosie's head. Allen cut the wire. The tension on the strand loosened and the necklace flew apart, beads tumbling everywhere. I grabbed Rosie under the arms to prevent her from sliding down the stairs and pulled her onto the balcony.

By now, the partiers downstairs had heard enough commotion to realize something was wrong. The music stopped, and people rushed to the bottom of the outside staircase that connected the balcony with the patio.

"Call 911!" I screamed. Rosie's eyes were closed and her face had turned pale blue. "Rosie? Rosie? Are you okay?" I put my ear to her chest. I thought I could hear a faint beating, but I couldn't tell if that was my own heart pounding, or hers. "I think she's still alive."

Tracy sat on the step next to her mother's limp body. "Mama. Mama, please be well, please be alive." She squeezed Rosie's hand, and it seemed to me Rosie squeezed back, but that may have been wishful thinking.

The ambulance arrived minutes later, and the medics went to work on Rosie, checking her vital signs, giving her an oxygen mask and starting an IV. Rosie was unconscious as the EMTs put a collar around her neck, placed her on a backboard, and carried her down the stairs. Rosie was alive, but in terrible shape. One of the paramedics told Allen the hospital would have to run tests and monitor her closely to make sure there was no permanent brain damage.

I watched the emergency technicians load Rosie into the ambulance, as all the other partygoers stood out of the way.

"Is anyone coming with us?" asked one of the medical technicians.

I looked at Tracy. She was in no shape to go to the hospital, unless she was the one being admitted.

"Look, I'm going to go with Rosie," I said, spotting Tessa. "Tracy, Tessa is going to get you settled so you can lie down upstairs." Tessa put her arm around Tracy and guided her back to the apartment. "I'll call you when I have an update," I said. This was the last thing I wanted to do tonight, but I knew it was the right thing.

"Allen, can you be a wonderful guy and help get the shop shut down and everyone sent home?"

"I am an expert at being a wonderful guy," Allen said with a smile, and I didn't doubt him. I also didn't doubt he was looking up my dress at my shiny black Spanx as I pulled myself into the back of the ambulance. I looked out the back window as we drove away. All of the partiers stood on the street watching us go, wondering what had happened.

FOURTEEN

THE STRETCHER, NOW RAISED up into a gurney, rolled into the emergency room at Virginia Mason Medical Center. Its huge glass-paneled façade gleamed brightly in the darkness. Since the emergency team had called ahead, there were doctors waiting for Rosie when she arrived.

"You the next of kin?" a nurse asked me.

"Uh, no, sorry, just a friend, you see—" The nurse interrupted me.

"You know what happened?"

"Well, you know—"

"Allergies?"

"She was strangled, so it's not like—"

"Medical hist—"

This time, it was my turn to cut her off.

"Look, I have very little information. I can tell you her name—Rosie, officially Rosa, I think, Paredes. A necklace was strangling her, and she couldn't breathe." The nurse raised a single eyebrow, but didn't look surprised. I'm certain she had heard it all, working in the ER.

"Unconscious when you found her?"

"I think she was conscious when I first saw her, but as I was helping her, she seemed to pass out."

"Can you describe the item that was around her neck?"

"A long strand of beads—it was wrapped tightly around her neck, so we cut the wire that held it together." I wondered if anyone would think to pick up the beads from the necklace, or if they had already been swept up and thrown away after the night's chaos, or taken by a greedy beader. Poor Rosie wouldn't want to lose her art glass bead collection.

"Wait here," said the nurse, turning on her heel, rubber soles squeaking as she walked away. They'd taken Rosie back through the double doors and into the treatment area. The nurse had stopped me before I'd been able to follow Rosie back.

I sat down on one of the vinyl benches in the waiting area, squeezing myself between a boy who looked like he'd been socked in the eye, along with a woman who was probably his mom, and a man who needed a few stitches on his finger, given the amount of blood soaked into the washcloth he was holding.

I stared in a daze at the blue-speckled tiles on the floor. I wanted to think, but my brain was on overload. I closed my eyes. My head was splitting, and a few realizations were dawning. It was the middle of the night. I had no money, no ID, no phone, and no way to get back to the shop, or home. I was stuck. Too bad this wasn't jail, because if it were, at least I'd get to make one phone call.

A nurse invited me back into the treatment room. Rosie was attached to several monitors, and I was shocked to see her looking so small and pale. Most of her face was obscured by a mask that was attached to oxygen tanks. They were pint-sized versions of what I used in the studio to power my torch.

"Are you here with Ms. Paredes?" the doctor asked. He seemed grim, and I was hoping that was his general mood rather than an indicator of how badly Rosie was doing. I nodded, and he continued. "I'm Dr. Patel, the doctor on duty tonight." He gave me a perfunctory handshake and offered me a seat near the foot of Rosie's bed.

"We are treating Ms. Paredes conservatively, given our concerns about her possible lack of oxygen," said Dr. Patel, as he sat down on a short stool and rolled over to me. "Can you tell me more about the circumstances of her accident?"

I filled him on the details of how I'd found Tracy and Rosie on the stairs, how I had seen Rosie struggle and pass out, that we had cut the necklace, and that the ambulance came soon after.

"Is she going to be okay?" I asked. It was a question I'm sure Dr. Patel heard many times a day.

"Her airway is open, and it appears there is no serious damage to her esophagus. I believe she lost consciousness for a period of time, but we do not think she stopped breathing entirely."

"I'm glad I found her when I did."

"Yes, she's a lucky woman to have a friend like you."

Friend? I suppose saving her life made me a friend.

"We're running a panel of tests, which will likely not reveal anything serious. She should have a full recovery. For now, however, we will be keeping her here for a day or two for observation and to complete our diagnostics."

"Okay, thanks, doctor," I said, stifling a yawn. I'm sure he could see how tired I was.

"And I suggest you go home and get some rest. There's nothing you can do here tonight."

I turned to leave, trying to figure out which door would get me back to the waiting room.

"Oh, and I'm curious," Dr. Patel said. "She had a series of unusual welts around her neck and some significant bruising. What kind of necklace would leave marks like that?"

"It was a necklace made of beads. Big, beautiful glass beads." I was too tired to explain any more. I found my way back to the lobby and straight out the door into the darkness.

The chilly air hit me and felt good on my face. Like a splash of cold water, it helped to clear my head. What I needed now was to get home. I saw a taxi on the corner and ran over to it. I was glad I had on my good Mary Janes tonight. I'd done more running, dancing, and rescuing in these shoes than I'd ever expected, all of which would have been more difficult in my tall heels.

A hefty African American woman was in the driver's seat. She didn't look like someone you'd want to mess with, and for a female cab driver, that was a good thing. I was hoping she'd take pity on me, a fellow woman in distress.

"Hi there," I said, flashing a broad grin. Mom always told me a smile was the best way to make a new friend, and right now, that was exactly what I needed. "I'm sort of stuck—I rode here to the hospital in an ambulance with someone and, well, I left without my handbag or my phone, so I don't have any way to get home."

"You drunk?" she asked bluntly, folding up the newspaper she'd been reading and tossing it onto a pile of garbage on the floor. I'm sure she often dealt with people trying to get home after a drunken bar brawl had left someone injured enough to require hospital treatment. I was a little insulted that she thought I looked like one of them.

"No, definitely not drunk. Look, my friend was hurt when she fell, and I rode with her in the ambulance. Can you please take me home? I have money there. I promise."

"Ya know how often I hear that? Couple times a night. Sometimes people are tellin' the truth, sometimes they're not. Right now, I'm not feelin' like being a trustin' person, ya know?"

"Look, I can give you..." I looked myself over. What did I have that I could give her? "My necklace. Do you like this?" I asked, as I unclasped it and handed it to her. She examined it carefully.

"What is this—plastic? Cheap crap made in China?"

"No, no, no. It's handmade. I made it. It's made of glass, in a torch, you see. I melt glass and then I add colors and clear glass in layers to make a design, and—"

"I like the color. Red. I think it'll be a nice addition to my wardrobe," she said, holding up the necklace to the black polo shirt stretched across her broad chest. I didn't care what she was going to wear it with, I just needed a ride. "I think it might look better on me than around your scrawny white neck."

"Yes. Totally. It looks great on you." I wouldn't have disagreed with her in any case, but I had to admit, it was a perfect necklace for her.

"Hop in."

I had never heard such beautiful words in my life.

A few minutes later, the taxi pulled up outside my house.

"Thanks for the ride," I said, as I slammed the door harder than necessary. I'd just given away one of my favorite necklaces in exchange for a 15-minute cab ride. Now I was standing at the front door of my house. And I didn't have any keys to get in. Dammit.

I rang Val's doorbell 10 times, and then I saw the entry light come on. I knew she was looking through the peephole at me. I gave her a little wave, and she yanked the door open.

"What on earth are you doing out here at 1 in the morning, sweet-cheeks?"

"There's too much to explain right now. I need sleep, and then we can talk."

"Val?" I heard a man's voice. "You going to come back? We've still got a few minutes left to watch on this movie."

"Who's in there? Don't tell me it's Rudy."

"Well, you see..." Val said, trying to find a good way to break the news to me.

I stared at her and said nothing.

"It's Rudy," she confessed.

"Rudy!" I'd been telling her she needed to try to look past outer beauty and consider the beauty within, but this seemed to be taking it to extremes. Rudy was the ugliest, scariest-looking guy I'd met in a long time. "And what, you're in there watching porno?"

"No. Not porno. I guess it's time for you to know the truth."

I stood on her doorstep, staring and waiting, not very patiently. It was way past my bedtime.

"I hate to admit this, but I love the *Star Wars* movies. They remind me of my childhood—Harrison Ford, all cute and everything. When Rudy came over yesterday, he was wearing this paint-splattered Han Solo T-shirt, and so we got talking," Val said. "After the party broke up early, I invited him over to watch one of the *Star Wars* DVDs. We're watching the first movie, which is actually the fourth one in the series. I just got the newest re-mastered edition—"

"Can we talk about your *Star Wars* obsession another day?"

You think you know someone. You live next door to them for a couple of years, and then you find out something completely random like this. Val was always surprising me. "I need your spare key," I said, leaning my forehead against the doorjamb. I was tired, and I wanted to go to bed.

"I don't have it, silly. I gave it to you earlier this evening to give to Marla, or Margo, or whatever the name is of that crazy woman with the dog."

"Marta." Of course. Marta was in the house. I knocked on the door, and waited. And waited.

"Where are you, Marta?" I grumbled, as I rang the bell and kicked the door with my foot, scuffing both my shoe and my door.

No answer.

I went around the side of the house and headed down the long alley between my house and Mr. Chu's. I usually left a key to the studio in a Hide-A-Key on the underside of the bistro table at the back door. It had been a long time since I'd used it, and I was thankful to find it still there. I let myself into the studio, not sure whether I needed to be quiet. I wondered if Marta was here, since she hadn't answered the door. Maybe she was still at the bead shop, although I doubted the party had kept going after Rosie's accident.

I heard the skittering of dog paws on the hardwood floor and the sound of galloping headed right for me. I was about to be hit in the knees by Stanley's head, followed by the full force of his squatty body.

"Stanley, sit!" I said, taking a complete leap of faith it would work. I'd seen Marta use the command earlier and hoped if I said it with enough conviction, it would work for me, too.

And it did. For the first time tonight, things were working as I'd hoped.

The sound of galloping dog feet ceased. I could see Stanley outlined in the doorway, the hallway light casting a long dog-shaped shadow onto my feet. I had stopped him in the nick of time.

"Stanley, stay!" I said. He flumped down on the ground, where I hoped he would stay all night. "Good boy," I said, reaching down and petting his head, to which he responded by slobbering all over my hand.

I went into my bedroom and closed the door, trying to shut out the night's memories: loud music, a tight strand of beads, Rosie's pale face, a speeding ambulance, a stark hospital, a grimy taxi, an annoying dog. I pulled off the red dress and tossed it in the trash. I didn't think I could ever wear that dress again, with all the bad memories it would bring back of this night. I put on my comfiest jammies and my fluffiest fleece socks and crept into bed, pulling one of Aunt Rita's patchwork quilts around me. It comforted me, as if she was here wrapping her arms around me. I wanted to stay there for the rest of my life, or at least until the sun was up, when daylight would make everything better. At least that's what I was hoping for.

FIFTEEN

TESSA WAS AT THE FRONT DOOR promptly at 9 o'clock in the morning, standing there with a large latte in one hand and a bag from Muffin Madness in the other.

"Tessa, you are my best friend," I said, taking the bag and giving her a big hug. I peeked inside. She'd brought me my favorite, a blueberry muffin.

"I thought you might want this," Tessa said, as she dropped my purse on the kitchen table.

"Thank you for rescuing my purse. It was hard getting home last night without it." Tessa had dark circles under her eyes. I wondered if she'd gotten much more sleep than I had.

"I bought an extra muffin for Marta," Tessa said, stifling a yawn.

"I'm not sure Marta's here. She didn't answer the door last night when I was pounding on it."

"What happened at the hospital? Is Rosie okay?"

I grabbed some plates and napkins, and we sat down at the round oak table.

"The doctor thought she was going to be fine. He's running some tests to make sure there's no permanent damage."

Marta shuffled out to the kitchen, looking bleary. Her green flannel nightgown covered in romping puppies was more than I could stand to look at this morning.

"Why didn't you answer the door last night?" I asked, feeling grumpy, my mouth half-full of muffin.

"What? Oh, wait...earplugs," said Marta, plucking them from her ears. "I can't hear a thing with them in. What did you say?"

"Never mind. I figured it out," I said, exasperated. "Muffin?"

"Do either of you know where Stanley is?" she said, rubbing her eyes and taking the muffin.

"Last time I saw him he was lying down in the studio," I told her, remembering the last "stay" command I'd given. That dog really knew how to obey if he was still in the same place this morning as he was last night.

Marta whistled far too loudly for this early in the morning, and Stanley came running, his long ears flipping lightly across the floor as he ran toward us. Perhaps I could have him run around the house to give the hardwoods a good dusting. At least that way he'd be useful.

I finished the muffin and coffee and sat looking across the table at Tessa. She jingled the keys in her hand. She was antsy.

"Tessa, do we need to be somewhere? I didn't think I had anything to do until tomorrow, when I have my workshop."

"I was at Aztec Beads until well after midnight trying to get things cleaned up," she said, "but at some point, I just gave up and went home. There's more to do to get the place ready for today's workshops. I'm not sure how Tracy is doing. And Judy might need some extra help so she doesn't have a meltdown."

Ah-ha! Tessa was here to recruit me. She figured if she brought me a muffin, I'd do anything for her. And she was probably right. I'd do almost anything for a good muffin. Throw in a large latte, and I'd be your slave for a day.

"If you're coming with me to help out at Aztec Beads, we should go. Pronto," Tessa said.

"Okay, let's go then," I said, grabbing my purse off the kitchen table and heading toward the front door.

"What? Wait!" said Tessa, alarmed.

"You said we needed to go to the shop, so let's go." I was tired, and I'd had a bad night, to put it mildly. I needed to keep moving; otherwise, I'd fall asleep.

"Jax? Have you noticed you're still in your pajamas?"

"Yes. It's my new fashion statement. Everyone is doing it these days, you know, wearing flannel PJ bottoms out and about," I said, doing a pirouette to show off the stylish outfit.

"Slippers? XXXL T-shirt with stains on it?"

I looked down at myself. Tessa had a point. I should not step outside looking like this. "Give me 15 minutes," I begged.

Fourteen-and-a-half minutes later, I was at the front door. I was wearing the same jeans I'd worn yesterday. But, desperate times, or lack of time, call for desperate measures. At least I'd been able to find a clean black T-shirt, and I'd thrown on my red clogs. Tessa was waiting for me, the keys still jingling in her hand.

Marta had finished her muffin and was sitting on the sofa, giving Stanley a good brushing.

"Are you headed over to Aztec Beads?" I asked her.

"In a little while. I don't want to miss Indigo's workshop."

"Sounds good; we'll see you over there."

"Jax, when you get back this afternoon, try and be real quiet, because Stanley will be taking his afternoon nap."

"Will do," I said, with a little inner eye-roll, and knowing the only reason I'd tiptoe around my own house was if I thought Gumdrop might come out of hiding if I was quiet. "Please keep your eyes open for Gumdrop," I added as I left.

I got into Tessa's van. It was a disaster area, full of soda cans, soccer uniforms, toys, a jumble of shoes favored by teen girls, ground-in dirt, and smudgy windows.

"Geez, Tessa, you need to clean the van out. It's a mess. Either that or just abandon this one and buy a new one. That may be a better option."

"Very funny. You try having three kids and keeping a car clean," Tessa said, looking ticked off and gripping the steering wheel tightly.

When we got to Aztec Beads, Tracy was sitting in her usual spot at the front of the shop, wringing a tissue between her hands. She looked more frail than usual. Like the rest of us, she probably hadn't slept much last night.

While I stopped to talk with Tracy, Tessa went straight to work, making sure the classroom would be ready for the first workshop.

"Hi, Tracy. How are you? How's your mom?" I asked softly, bending down to make eye contact. Tracy's face was half-hidden by her long dark hair.

"I called the hospital this morning, and they said Mama was sedated. I couldn't talk with her. The nurse who answered the phone said they were still running tests."

"Oh, I am so sorry. The good news is your mom is alive, and the doctors are doing everything they can to help her," I said, reaching across the counter to give her a big squeeze on the shoulders, the best hug I could manage with a display case between us.

Tracy pulled a new tissue out of the sleeve of her sweater, old-lady-style, and wiped her puffy eyes.

"I think you need to go over to the hospital and see your mom," I suggested.

"But she won't know I'm there."

"Well, do it for *you*, then. Go on over to the hospital, and Tessa and I will clean up. It's still a wreck around here. We'll get things all cleaned up and handle any customers. Judy will be here soon, and she can keep the workshops going. But we'd better get moving. We've got jewelry-making demos starting in an hour, I think."

Without saying another word, Tracy took her purse and headed out the door.

"Looks like there's a lot to do around here," I said, seeing two over-stuffed bags of garbage by the back door. I grabbed the bags and headed out onto the back porch. Fortunately, someone had taken the time to clean up the yard. It was back to normal, other than the small patch of grass that had been trampled last night by danc-ing partygoers, myself included. I dragged the bags out the back gate and down the long alley, where a banged-up green Dumpster sat near the edge of the building.

I opened the top of the large trash bin and threw in one of the sacks. I released the bag and then the lid. A puff of stench hit my face as the black lid slammed down.

I opened the lid again, getting ready to throw the other bag in. Something caught my eye. A thin piece of red fabric was caught on the front lip of the bin. Somehow, that small thing set off an alarm in me. I looked inside the Dumpster. Under a pile of paper plates and leftover potato chips, I saw a worn red flannel shirt, a tangle of long matted hair, then part of a delicate hand, and a tiny geometric pattern tattooed on a wrist. Still and lifeless.

"Oh, God!" I yelled, dropping the lid and the garbage sack. I ran down the alley and found Tessa in the yard. "Help!" I screamed between gulps of air, as I started pulling her out the gate.

"Jax, use your words," Tessa demanded. "What's wrong?"

"Dead. A dead, a body...dead..." I choked on the words.

"Oh, Jax, I know it seems like there's some scary stuff in the Dumpster, but a dead body? Seriously. Your imagination is running wild. Maybe someone threw away a mannequin," said Tessa, leaving my side and marching down the alley.

"Go check for yourself; I can't look again. I'm calling 911." I stumbled back to the edge of the porch and sat down, my legs almost collapsing beneath me. Above me, just hours ago, Rosie had nearly died.

"Emergency Dispatch," said the 911 operator on the line. "Location?"

"The corner of Emerald Avenue and 45th Northeast."

"Name?"

"Jax O'Connell."

"Can you state the nature of the emergency, Ms. O'Connell?"

Tessa, pale as a sheet, ran toward me, crossing herself over and over. "Dio Mio, Jax!" Tessa's Italian always bubbled out of her mouth in times of stress. "There's a young woman in the Dumpster, and she's dead! Morti! Dio Mio!"

"Did you hear what my friend just told me?" I asked the dispatcher.

"Yes, ma'am, I did. Officers are on their way."

I hung up. Tessa sank down onto the steps next to me. In shock, we did the only thing we could. We hugged each other tight, giving and receiving comfort wordlessly as only friends can do.

"It's Misty," Tessa said. "Her red shirt."

I could feel warm tears streaming down my cheek. My face was pressed so close to Tessa's, I wasn't sure whose tears they were.

SIXTEEN

THE POLICE SPENT the morning with the alley cordoned off. They conducted a full crime scene inspection, bagged evidence, dusted for fingerprints, and did all the usual things that happen when there's been a murder. I couldn't watch. It was too upsetting.

A detective found me inside Aztec Beads. I was doing my best to look like I knew what to do in the store, and had taken over Tracy's spot at the front counter. I thought I was faking it extremely well.

"Good morning, ma'am, I'm Detective Grant," said the man, extending his hand. He looked younger than me. His hair was slicked back in an old-school style, and he wore dark heavy-framed glasses, which made him look older than he likely was. He was trying to be pleasant, but I could see a bit of a sneer on his lips.

"Nice to meet you, Grant," I said, extending my hand.

"Grant is my last name. You can call me *Detective* Grant." Too bad this guy was so prickly. With a new hairstyle, and maybe a less ugly tie, he'd be cute, in that Clark Kent sort of way. Val's penchant for makeovers was definitely rubbing off on me.

"Jax O'Connell. Nice to meet you, Detective Grant," I said, trying to fix my lack of decorum with a "re-do" by offering him my hand a second time. He opened his leather notebook and declined my second offer to shake.

"I understand you found the deceased," Detective Grant said, clicking his pen and starting to write.

"Yes, I found her in the Dumpster," I said.

"Can you describe how you found the body?"

"I opened the trash bin, and I saw her under some garbage." I looked toward the classroom, where a few people in the audience were craning their necks to see what was happening with the police detective in the shop.

"Can we please go outside? I think having you here in the shop may be causing a distraction in the class going on in the next room," I said.

"Did you know Misty Carlton?" the detective asked. We squeezed our way out the back door between racks hung with hundreds of strands of beads, the displays twirling as we brushed by.

Once outside, I felt more at ease and able to talk more freely. It had started to rain again, and we stood under the balcony, trying to keep dry. "I'd talked with her a few times at Fremont Fire. She used to work on the torches in the studio there. And I saw her here at the store."

"In the store?"

"Out in front of it, selling her beads on the street with her partner, Nick." I watched as the detective scribbled something in his notebook. "Detective Grant, was Misty murdered?"

"At this point we are investigating this case as a homicide, based on the medical examiner's on-site evaluation. Do you know anyone who would have wanted to harm this young woman?"

"The only person I can think of was rushed to the hospital last night," I said.

"When was the last time you saw Misty Carlton alive?"

"Last night before the party. So I guess that means she died last night." Suddenly, I was feeling defensive. The detective made me nervous. He looked at me with well-practiced patience, waiting for me to expose some detail of the murder only the killer would know.

I was sure he considered everyone he talked to at a crime scene to be suspects. I suppose that's what made him a good detective—if he was one, that is.

It was chilly outside, and I pulled my denim jacket around me. *Did pulling my jacket closed make me look guilty?* I hoped not. I hoped it just made me look cold. I glanced out the gate and down the alley. I couldn't see the trash bin from where I stood, but could hear a truck rumbling. The police were removing the Dumpster, and Misty was on her way to the morgue. The thought made me shiver.

"And who is the person who was supposedly 'in the hospital' when Ms. Carlton was fatally wounded?"

"Rosie Paredes. She owns this shop, and she's the one person I can think of who might want to harm Misty. But I can't imagine that she'd have the capacity to kill someone." Was he questioning whether she was actually in the hospital? I'd been there with Rosie, and she'd spent the night. I was her alibi, along with all the partygoers at the shop, and the doctors and nurses who treated her. Fortunately for Rosie, hospital records would back that up.

"Do you know what time Ms. Paredes went to the hospital last night?"

"I don't know, sometime after 11, I think." I was trying to remember what time it was when I knocked on Val's door. One in the morning? Had I been at the hospital for an hour? Longer? I couldn't figure it out right now in my sleep-deprived state.

"The medical examiner completed an initial assessment at the crime scene and is setting the time of death at midnight, based on Ms. Carlton's state of rigor mortis."

"But if Misty was killed much later than 11, then it couldn't be Rosie, right? Isn't there a way to determine the time of death more accurately?"

"We'll be doing a toxicology analysis and determining a more accurate time and cause of death, as well as any other assessments regarding the status of the deceased."

"Like whether she had drugs in her system?"

"Yes, it's a routine test, especially in situations like this in which we have a homeless person who—"

"I'm not sure she was homeless," I said, trying to explain Misty's situation. "Just not fully-homed."

Detective Grant looked at me skeptically over the top of his notebook as I continued.

"She is—was," I corrected, "an artist, and young. Sometimes it's hard making ends meet." I was thinking about Dylan, and how hard he worked just to pay his rent.

"Our assumption at this point is that she was killed in the alley. Do you know what she was doing back there?" Detective Grant asked.

"No idea. There were appetizers on the patio during the party. Maybe she came by to help herself to leftovers after the party had ended."

"Or maybe she came to score some drugs in the alley, and ended up dead."

"I think I like the idea of looking for food better."

"So, this person you think had a motive to kill Misty, what's her name? Rosie?"

"Rosie Paredes," I said, hating to implicate her in a murder while she was in the hospital, and having come so close to death herself just hours before.

"Did you ever see Ms. Paredes threaten the victim?"

"No. She was angry with Misty and her partner, but I'm not sure she ever had any direct contact with them," I said. While Rosie never had much to do with Misty, I wondered whether Tracy had. Could Rosie have coerced Tracy into killing Misty? It was too painful to imagine.

"Her daughter, Tracy. You should probably talk with her," I said as I held back tears.

"Who else are you aware of who knew the deceased?" the detective pressed on.

"The only other person I can think of is Dylan. He knew Misty from the Fremont Fire studio. Oh, and Nick, Misty's partner. But I don't think either of them would have killed her."

"Ah, yes, Fremont Fire. That's Tessa Ricci's business. Ms. Ricci was with you when you found the body, correct?" asked the detective. "I've talked with her, and she has assured me she will pass on the contact information of those individuals to me. Most likely it isn't anyone who knew the girl, just some random junkie who wanted her drugs or money. These drug-related murders are a low priority for us, so you shouldn't expect any closure on this any time soon."

"Did she have drugs on her?"

"A few grams of cannabis. Not illegal here in Washington, but it certainly means the circumstances of her death are clouded by this discovery. She also had a great deal of pale powdery substance under her fingernails. Could be methamphetamine. We've been seeing a large number of meth deals gone wrong recently, and someone often ends up dead."

"Detective, do you know about last night's accident here?" He looked at me blankly, and I filled him in on what had happened to Rosie.

Grant listened, but he didn't take any notes.

"Maybe Rosie's fall wasn't an accident," I said. "Maybe someone was trying to murder her, too." All this talk of murder had made me wonder about what happened last night with Rosie on the balcony.

"Miss, what we have here is the killing of a drug addict, and a woman who slipped on some wet stairs and choked when her necklace caught on the bannister. Frankly, I think you've been watching a few too many crime shows. Now, unless you have any additional information, I need to get back to the real world here."

Finding a dead girl in a Dumpster felt pretty real to me.

"Okay, I'll be in touch if I think of anything else."

"You'd better be," he warned. He wrote down his phone number, ripped it from his notebook, and handed it to me.

The police department must have cut their business card budget. I stuffed the scrap in my pocket and found the bead I'd bought from Misty. I pulled it out and admired it. It was full of creative beauty, as Misty had been.

The detective closed his notebook, a sure sign he was done with me. I watched him walk back down the alley and duck under the crime-scene tape.

"Detective, can I ask you one thing?" I called out, as I watched him saunter down the alley.

"You can ask, but it doesn't mean I'll answer," he said over his shoulder, still walking. Too bad he was such a jerk, because he had a cute butt.

"How did Misty die?"

"She was strangled with some sort of flat cord."

SEVENTEEN

I CLOSED THE GATE so Rosie's dog wouldn't escape. I hadn't seen that little monster this morning. He was probably upstairs hiding from the chaos. Tessa came up behind me and I could smell the coffee she was holding. Like one of Pavlov's dogs, I felt like drooling. "I zipped out and got you some coffee," she said, handing me a large latte.

A thick mist was pressing down on us, in typical Seattle style. We sat on the steps under the balcony so our butts didn't get wet sitting at the patio table.

"What's going on?" Tessa asked, taking a sip of her espresso.

"The detective," I said nodding in the direction of the alley, "not that nice." I took a big gulp of coffee. Hot and sweet, just the way I liked it.

"I talked with him earlier," she told me. "He wants to talk with Nick and Dylan."

"Right. In fact, he thinks she was killed in a drug deal. What do you think—could she have been trying to score some drugs?"

Tessa looked me straight in the eye, as certain as I've ever seen her. "No, Jax. She wasn't using drugs, at least not anything more than pot. I helped Misty and Nick. A lot. I made it clear to them

I wouldn't support them in any way if they were going to do any serious drugs. And I believe they respected that rule."

I didn't doubt it for a minute. You did not want to cross Tessa. Her fiery Italian attitude kept almost everyone in line, except for me. She'd given up trying to keep me in order.

"So it doesn't it make sense to you that Misty was killed in a drug deal?"

"No. Not at all."

"What about Nick? Could he—?"

"Could Nick have killed her? No, I can't imagine it," Tessa said. "He cared about Misty. She'd helped him get focused and turn his life around. And, for all his tough exterior, he is a stand-up guy."

"What about Dylan?" I asked.

"There's no reason to suspect him that I can think of. He knew Misty from my studio. I never saw any tension or arguments between them," said Tessa, tipping back the rest of her drink.

"Maybe there was something there we don't know about? Maybe Dylan and Misty had a relationship."

"Misty and Nick were partners. I can't see Dylan involved in some sort of a love triangle, can you? Besides, Dylan had known Nick for a long time, so it's hard to imagine Dylan would have wanted to ruin that friendship."

"But Dylan did come in the back gate last night. He was in the alley around the time Misty was killed."

"I don't like where you're headed with this, Jax."

"The detective said Misty was strangled," I said. "Dylan did have a belt on last night, you know. Val gave it to him to wear to the party. It was a strap that could have been used to strangle Misty."

"I'd say at least half the people at the party had belts on, Jax. I doubt we can rule out anyone wearing saggy pants as the murderer."

Tessa was right. It could have been anyone at the party, or it could have been, as the detective believed, a stranger who killed Misty for drugs or money.

Tessa, shifting away from my ridiculous belt theory, continued. "Frankly, the biggest suspect I see is Rosie. She was completely irrational about Misty and Nick being in competition with her. I wish she could have seen them as two decent people trying to survive, and not trying to undermine her business," Tessa said.

"Rosie was in the hospital with me last night. There's no way she could be the killer," I said. "Maybe Grant—"

"Detective Grant," corrected Tess.

"Whatever," I growled. I was starting to sound like Izzy and Ashley. "Maybe the police haven't correctly calculated the time Misty died. The detective did say they were going to do some additional tests. Maybe they'll be able to pinpoint the time she died more accurately, and that will help him figure out what happened."

I gazed out at the gray sky in hopes of seeing a ray of sunshine, perhaps one that might shed some light on our puzzling and tragic situation.

"Tell me what happened last night with Rosie."

I paused a long time before I answered, visualizing what I had seen when I found Rosie and Tracy. I wanted to make sure I got it right.

"It was dark on the balcony. The only light was coming from below, and from the lights that had been hung in the trees. When I came around the corner from the kitchen, Rosie was on her back, feet-first down the staircase. Her head was at a strange angle, not touching the top step—suspended." I took a deep breath. "Her arms were moving, grabbing above her head," I said, closing my eyes and trying to remember every detail. "I saw Tracy next to Rosie, trying to help her mom up. No one else was there. Tracy was screaming, but the music below us was so loud, no one could hear her."

Tessa was silent. She squeezed my hand, knowing that small gesture was a way to comfort me, and a way to tell me she was listening as I tried to relive the painful moment.

"At first I couldn't see the necklace. It was too dark. Rosie was reaching for something, and then I finally saw the strand. I tried to unhook the necklace from the balcony's railing, but it wouldn't budge. When Allen arrived and cut the wire, Rosie's head hit the top step as the tension that held her up was released. All the beads went flying. She slid down a few steps, and I grabbed her and pulled her back onto the landing. By then, everyone on the patio had realized something was wrong and had gathered at the bottom of the stairs."

"I can't believe she fell like that. Those stairs must have been wet and slick."

"They didn't seem slippery to me."

Tessa continued, ignoring me. "It could have happened to any of us, falling on the stairs like that."

"I suppose you're right." And while I agreed with her that anyone could have fallen, all I could think about was that the stairs had not been slick. I'd been down on my knees helping Rosie, and my legs weren't wet when I stood up. It had been raining earlier, but an awning covered most of the stairs, so they were dry.

"Tessa? What if it wasn't an accident? Two people were strangled just a few hours apart."

"That's just a coincidence, Jax. Nobody here is a killer."

"But if Rosie's 'accident' was really an attempt to murder her, then we'd be looking for two killers." I swirled the last of the coffee around in the cup. Like a mystic reading tea leaves, I wondered if I could read coffee grounds. I doubted it.

"Suddenly *we're* looking for killers? We? As in, you and me?" Tessa asked incredulously.

"Yes. *We*, because, as you can see, Grant—or Detective Grant, or whatever his official name is—doesn't seem to be looking for any killers."

"And maybe we shouldn't be looking for any, either," said Tessa, being annoyingly rational. "Maybe you should slow down that creative mind for a minute and consider that the detective might actually be right. Rosie was injured in an accident, and Misty died in a situation completely unrelated to us."

"You're right. I've got a pretty wild imagination," I said, sipping the last of my now-cold coffee from the bottom of the cup.

"And that creative mind is what makes you such a fabulous glass artist."

"Artist?"

"Absolutely."

"Thanks. It's been a long time since someone told me that," I said. Jerry had said it once.

• • •

I'd go down to the scientific glass-blowing shop in the basement of our research facility at Clorox to watch Jerry work. His job was to make custom glassware for research and product development projects. At times, he worked with a small torch attached to his workbench, making precise parts for a distillation system. At other times, he worked at a huge lathe, which spun glass tubes around while a giant ring of flame heated the glass from all sides so it could be formed into larger-scaled scientific apparatus. Visiting Jerry while he was working with hot glass in the lab was the most exciting part of my day. I loved going down and watching him work. I never knew what he'd be making, but no matter what it was, it always fascinated me.

One day I was watching Jerry make some long thumb-sized cylinders. He was doing something he called "pulling points," forming inch-long, clear pea-pod shapes in the torch from glass tubing. A pile of them sat on his workbench.

They looked like soap bubbles, and I'd thought it would be fun to make a necklace out of them.

"Can you make those into beads, you know, with a hole at each end?" I asked Jerry.

"Sure, that's easy. It's one of the first things you learn to do in scientific glass blowing."

"Make beads?"

"Make holes in glass tubes."

"Can you add colors to these glass pods?" I asked, as I picked one up to admire it.

"I suppose so," Jerry said, trying to humor me while concentrating on his work.

"Can we try it sometime?"

"Ah, Jax, always an artist, trying to figure out new ways to be creative."

• • •

Tessa pulled me back into the present. "Jax? Earth to Jax."

"Sorry," I said, jumping up.

"Let's get out of here. I need to get things back to normal at Fremont Fire after yesterday's demos. Craig's dropping Izzy and Ashley off there so they can help us."

I stuck my head in the back door of the shop. Judy was starting the next workshop of the day. She looked as sweaty as ever. Her gray bangs hung like damp curtains across her forehead, and her bifocals were sliding down her nose. With Rosie in the hospital and Tracy gone to visit her, Judy was left to keep the classes moving along.

"Okay, everyone," said Judy, waving her clipboard around and fanning herself at the same time, "right now we have a demo with Indigo Martin. She'll be showing you how to create this lovely necklace made from her own handmade glass leaf beads."

Could Judy have tried to strangle Rosie? She'd been at the party — it was one of the most important events of the weekend, with a dozen fellow JOWL members in attendance. But, what about Misty? Was there any reason Judy would've wanted to kill her, too?

"I can hear you thinking," said Tessa. "And no, I don't think Judy had any reason to kill Misty, or Rosie."

"Are you sure? Menopause can make women do crazy things."

"True, although I would not know from *personal* experience," Tessa said with a laugh.

I waved at Judy as she turned things over to Indigo, to let her know I was taking off.

Judy waved back and smiled, and we headed out the front door and back to Fremont Fire.

EIGHTEEN

"THE FIRST THING I want you to do is to put all of the chairs back in the storage room." Tessa was addressing her two teen daughters. Both girls looked at their mother, and sighed with contempt, their arms crossed, not moving.

"Go!" Tessa shouted.

The girls knew their mom meant business and figured they couldn't resist any longer. They started pulling on chairs, legs scraping and screeching across the floor as they dragged them into the closet.

"Girls! Please *pick up* the chairs and carry them," bossed Tessa.

Izzy rolled her eyes and lifted a chair. She carried it into the closet and dropped it loudly. In the storage room, Izzy and Ashley bumped shoulders, each crying "OW!" as they passed. I'm pretty sure they had bumped shoulders on purpose to injure each other.

Ah, siblings, can't live with 'em, can't kill 'em. Or something like that. It had certainly been a problem with my sister Connie and me. We'd fought all the time, over stupid things like who got to sit on which side of the car. Not who got to ride shotgun, but whether sitting behind the passenger's or the driver's seat was better. It would get so bad at times my mother would take off her shoe and threaten us with it from the front seat. This wasn't intimidating, since she was wearing flip-flops most of the time.

The fighting lessened eventually, especially when our little brother was with us. We were so busy adoring Andy we almost forgot to fight with each other. Izzy and Ashley were like that, too, whenever their little brother was around.

"What do you want me to do?" I asked, finally perking up from my last round of coffee.

"It would help a lot if you could put away all of the extra supplies and tools we used yesterday. That way, we'll be back to business as usual around here."

I looked around Tessa's studio. What a terrific place. I'd spent a lot of time here since I'd moved to Seattle, and Tessa had taught me so much. When I first arrived, I'd only known how to work with borosilicate glass. It's what Jerry used at Clorox, and what he eventually taught me to use. Tessa taught me how to use a completely different kind of glass, from Italy. The Italian glass was amazing, available in almost every color you could imagine. I loved the way this beautiful glass moved in the flame when I melted it with my torch.

As for Tessa, glass flowed in those Italian veins of hers. She'd been born in Italy before moving to Florida, where I met her when we were both six. She'd moved back to Italy again for a while after high school. Her parents wanted to make sure she got an American education, she'd told me on more than one occasion. I think her parents had hoped that when she moved back to Italy after high school, she'd stay there for the rest of her life. They didn't plan on Tessa meeting the love of her life, darling Craig. Tessa's parents had hoped she'd find a nice Italian boy to settle down with, not an American who just happened to be visiting Murano when he met Tessa. Within a year of meeting, they'd fallen madly in love and moved to Seattle to be close to his family.

Tessa loved living in Seattle, one of the best cities in the world for art glass. It was home to Dale Chihuly and to many other amazing glass artists. There was a glass museum, countless galleries, and one of the best glass schools in the nation, if not the world. Some would say Seattle is more significant to the glass world than Venice, with many leading-edge artists and designers pushing the limits of what can be created with glass. Although Tessa was here in Seattle, I knew her heart still belonged to Venice.

"Mom! Izzy's not working, she's texting," complained Ashley, from the storage room.

We could hear an argument brewing.

"MOM! Izzy called me the 'B' word."

"Izzy, bring me your phone," Tessa said, squeezing her eyes shut.

"What? No way. This is my phone."

"Did you buy it with your own money? Do you pay the monthly fees?"

"No," Izzy said, arms crossed.

"Then would you say that it is *your* phone?"

"No," said Izzy, deflated. "Don't read my messages, okay?"

"I won't read your messages. Just put it in this drawer." Tessa slid open the drawer under the cash register.

Izzy's phone dropped with a clunk into the drawer, and Izzy gave her mother the "look of death" as she passed by her.

Back in the storage room, Izzy and Ashley continued working, with only minor grumbling.

We finished the last little bit of cleanup and were ready to go.

"All right. Excellent job," said Tessa. "I want to get back over to Aztec Beads to watch some of the classes. I need to learn something this weekend, and not just how to avoid being the next victim of the notorious necklace strangler."

"Actually, Mom, I was hoping I could use your car," said Izzy. "You know, like maybe Jax can give you a ride home?"

"You want my car?" Tessa asked, hands on hips.

"Yes, please," said Izzy, smiling sweetly and, frankly, unconvincingly, trying her best to look like an angel.

"What are you going to *do* with my car?"

"Drive around, go to Dick's Burgers, shop at Northgate Mall," said Izzy, as if she were trying to explain something as natural and simple as breathing.

Ashley glared darkly at her sister, knowing she had to babysit again tonight. Tessa had magnanimously offered to keep Benny for the rest of the weekend after Rosie's accident—or attempted murder, depending on your point of view.

"I am not going to pick up any boys," Izzy promised. I wasn't sure there were many boys who would have wanted to be seen in a 10-year-old minivan, especially one that needed to be blasted with a pressure-washer, inside and out. But, then again, a cute 16-year-old girl behind the wheel of the van could overcome all sorts of obstacles.

"Fine," Tessa said. "Then you can do me a favor. Drop your sister home for me. Your dad took Joey and Benny to the aquarium, but I'm sure by the time they get back, he's going to want a break. Ashley's on babysitting duty tonight."

"Okay," Izzy said, grabbing the keys from Tessa's hand. Ashley was unhappy about the situation, but she knew there was no way she'd be allowed to go with her sister tonight.

"And no stopping!" Tessa yelled as the girls headed for the door.

Izzy stopped and turned around. "Not even at the stop signs? Mom, I don't think that would be safe." she said.

"Smarty pants!" I yelled at them with a smile.

My phone rang, but I didn't recognize the number. Maybe it was Rudy finally calling to give me an estimate on painting the kitchen.

"Hello, Ms. O'Connell." I recognized the stiffness in the caller's voice immediately. "This is Detective Grant, Seattle PD. I'm trying to locate Tessa Ricci. Do you know how I might reach her?"

"She's standing right here next to me," I told him. "And Detective, have you thought any more about Rosie? That what happened to her may have been more than an accident? Because I think—"

"Ms. O'Connell. I am the investigator on this case. I am investigating," Detective Grant said as he shut me down.

"Oh. Okay. Right," I said, ready to hang up the phone.

"Ms. O'Connell? May I please speak to Ms. Ricci? Now."

Tessa's eyes were popping out, alarmed that the detective was calling for her.

"Oh, yes, sorry. Here she is."

"Yes, hello?" said Tessa, trying to act calm, cool, and collected. Fortunately, Detective Grant couldn't see Tessa's bulging eyes, which looked, at that moment, like the eyes of Rosie's little dog, Tito.

"Of course, yes," Tessa continued. "Okay. Yes. Yes." It was hard to tell what was happening from Tessa's side of the conversation, other than she was being agreeable. She hung up the phone.

"Jax, this is not good. Detective Grant wants me at his office right now."

"Is he going to arrest you?" I asked.

"No, silly, but he does want to talk with me."

"Why you? Does he think you have something to do with Misty's murder?"

"Who knows, but we better get down there."

We dashed out the door and onto the street.

"Where's the Ladybug?" we both said simultaneously.

"GAH!" again simultaneously.

We'd both come to the same realization at the same moment: We had sent the girls off in Tessa's car. *Our only form of transportation.*

The Ladybug was back at my house. Neither Tessa nor I had gotten enough sleep last night, and we were not thinking clearly.

"Tessa, you just gave away your car," I said.

"How could I be so stupid? I'm not running on all cylinders. How are we supposed to get to the police station?" Tessa asked. "We could walk. It would take an hour. Or the bus?"

"I'm calling a cab," I decided. "It worked for me last night. But I had to give the driver one of my best necklaces for cab fare, since I didn't have my purse."

"You gave away the red necklace? You loved that piece," said Tessa.

"I loved the idea of getting home last night even more," I told her. "I can make another one."

The taxi rolled up in front of Fremont Fire a few minutes later. The driver rolled down her window.

"You again?" It was the same hefty driver from last night. She looked at my necklace, a tiny glass ladybug on a silver chain, scoping it out to see if I might want to trade.

"Sorry, I've got real money today, so I don't need to barter."

"That's a damn shame, b'cause I really am liking that necklace you gave me," the driver said.

"Well, enjoy it," I said with a sigh, as I swung myself onto the sticky back seat next to Tessa.

"Where to?"

"Downtown Police Department," Tessa said, getting down to business in her usual direct manner.

"You sure you're not in trouble? Because last night I was sensin' trouble, and now you're going to see the cops."

"No," said Tessa, with an edge to her voice. "We just have some, uh, business to take care of."

"Oh, yeah, I know *that* kind of *business*. I've bailed out my cousin a couple times down there at the station."

"We are not trying to get someone out of jail," Tessa insisted.

"We are trying to *keep* someone out of jail," I told Tessa, as I poked her in the arm.

About 20 minutes later, we were sitting in a stuffy conference room at the Seattle Police Department. It was decorated with early-'70s orange chairs and mustard-yellow carpeting mottled with dark brown stains. Coffee spills, no doubt. Just thinking about coffee made me want a cup. After only a few hours of sleep, coffee sounded fantastic right now. Well, coffee sounded good to me almost any time.

The detective agreed to let me stay in the conference room with Tessa as long as I didn't say anything. Clearly, he didn't know me, because he'd have known it was impossible for me to keep quiet for any extended period of time.

Detective Grant took a seat, looking at us with half a scowl. I felt like I'd shrunk in my seat when he stared at us across the table.

The detective started with an excellent question.

"Where is the necklace that Ms. Paredes was wearing last night?"

"I don't know," Tessa said. "The last time I saw it, Rosie was wearing it. When Jax was trying to save Rosie, a friend of hers cut the wire that held the necklace together, and the beads scattered everywhere. I guess they were swept away when everyone cleaned up." I stayed quiet, as instructed, but mostly by clenching my lips together.

"Isn't that strange? These nice beads, they must have been valuable," Detective Grant mused.

"Yes—" I started, but before I could continue, I felt a sharp pain on the top of my foot as Tessa stepped down on it, hard.

"Yes, they'd be worth maybe a thousand, or 1,500 dollars. But, really, they were priceless, because it would be nearly impossible to replace all of those beads. They were handmade, each by a different artist," Tessa said.

"I wonder if someone would steal them because their fingerprints were on the beads—fingerprints of the person who tried to kill Rosie Paredes," pondered Grant. "Perhaps by stealing them, the person was covering their tracks."

"Everyone touches—" I started, and again Tessa stomped on my foot.

"Detective, you see," said Tessa, trying to figure out how to say what I had almost blurted out, "people who love beads, they all touch each other's necklaces. They don't really ask, they just come up to someone and admire their jewelry by picking up a bead on a strand and examining it closely. It happens all the time."

Detective Grant looked at Tessa like she was a crazy person. "This means there would be many different sets of prints on the beads?"

"Yes."

"Even your own?"

"I didn't touch the necklace last night. Since one of my beads was on the strand, that one might have my fingerprints on it," Tessa told him.

Dammit. I most definitely had admired the beads on Rosie's necklace. I'd picked up a few to examine them closely. In a strange way, it was good those beads were missing. Otherwise, I might have been the next one being grilled by the detective.

"Tell me," said Detective Grant, "are you unhappy Ms. Paredes opened her shop so near your studio?"

"No. I am not unhappy," Tessa answered. "Which is really like saying, that yes, I am happy. Well not happy, but not *not* happy. Just sort of neutral."

Geez, Tessa was starting to sound like me, unable to put together a complete sentence under stress.

"According to Tracy Paredes, your shop carries items that are similar to items in Aztec Beads."

"What?"

"Miss Paredes indicated she was in your place of business yesterday, and she saw many items in the front window that were nearly identical to what is carried in her mother's new store," Detective Grant explained.

"No, actually, it's not that way at all. I'm really glad they opened," said Tessa, through tight lips. She sounded guilty, although I knew she wasn't. "We complement each other. I carry handmade lamp-worked beads, and when someone buys something at my studio, I send them to Aztec Beads to buy what they need to finish their jewelry project by purchasing additional beads, clasps, and other components, like wire, that I don't carry."

"But you saw them as competition?" said the detective, prodding her.

"Well, no, not really. I suppose they have some things that I have, but..." Tessa trailed off. I tried to send her my best psychic signals, telling her to stand up for herself. Too bad Gumdrop wasn't here—he could have sent her messages with his psychic abilities.

"Where were you last night between 11 and 1?"

"At the party at Aztec Beads," Tessa said.

"You were there when Ms. Paredes was hurt?"

The detective was on his way to concluding that Tessa was at the party when Rosie was strangled, and that she'd had the opportunity and the motive to try to kill her.

"If you're thinking I tried to kill Rosie, well, that is just not true," Tessa said.

I knew Detective Grant was jumping to the wrong conclusion, but as he had told me earlier, he was investigating this crime, not me. I kept quiet.

"From what I can put together, the party ended around 11:30, after Ms. Paredes was injured. And when Rosie Paredes was on her way to the hospital, where were you then?"

"At Aztec Beads, cleaning up."

"Cleaning up? You mean, putting things in the Dumpster?"

"Yes, I put some things in there," Tessa said matter-of-factly. The detective was painting another clear picture: that Tessa had also killed Misty. She'd had the opportunity last night when she was cleaning up.

"And what time did you leave?"

"I'm not sure what time. It was pretty late. Maybe 1 in the morning?" Tessa's timing was terrible. She was at Aztec Beads at midnight, the time estimated by the medical examiner of Misty's death.

"Who else was there?"

"Allen Sinclair was there, helping get the place closed up for the night."

"Just a couple more questions," said Detective Grant. "Tell me about Misty Carlton."

"She was a young woman who made lampworked beads, and rented time to work at a torch in my studio."

"Yes, Tracy Paredes said you have some sort of flame-throwing studio."

"Flameworking," Tessa clarified. "Just a small flame, not a giant one."

I bit my lips harder, trying not to laugh. I knew someday we'd be able to joke about flame-throwers, but today wasn't the day.

"And did Ms. Carlton always pay her rental fees?" asked Detective Grant.

"Sometimes she paid, and sometimes she didn't quite have enough money." Tessa's generosity was about to get her in serious trouble.

"Would you say she owed you a large sum of money?"

"I think over the last year, it added up to maybe 800 dollars, but I didn't mind at all. She is—was—a sweet girl, and I wanted to help her, and her partner, Nick." Because I knew Tessa so well, I could hear the tiniest pinch in her voice. I could tell how hard she was trying to keep her tears from spilling out.

"But she did owe you a great deal of money?" Grant asked the question again, more intensely, trying to unnerve my friend.

"Not a lot, but yes, she owed me money. I guess it was a lot," said

Tessa, trying to be honest.

"Enough money to want to kill her?" the detective asked harshly.

"NO!" said Tessa, losing her cool and jumping up.

The detective stood as well. Protectively, I stood up, too, and moved to stand closer to Tessa.

"Until you showed up on my radar, Ms. Ricci, I thought Ms. Paredes's injury was an accident and Ms. Carlton was killed for drugs. Now, I'm not so sure what we're looking at."

He opened the door and stepped aside so we could leave. Tessa grabbed her purse and slung it onto her shoulder. I saw the detective take a long look at the strap.

On the steps of the police station, Tessa called Craig and filled him in on what had happened. While Tessa was on the phone, I saw Detective Grant come out of the front doors of the building. One thing puzzled me. It was the way he'd asked about where Tessa had been between 11 and 1 last night.

I took a chance and followed him down the steps.

"Detective Grant, can I ask you a question? I swear I'm not trying to be a super-sleuth. It's just a question about timing."

He stopped, looking at me like an angry bull. I plunged ahead. "If Misty died at midnight, why did you ask Tessa where she was between 11 and 1?"

He stood there, looking at me darkly. I swear his foot was scuffing the ground like he was ready to charge.

Finally, he answered impatiently. "Because we can't pinpoint a death down to the minute. Without any test results, the medical examiner can't say she died at exactly 12:02. It's always a range: Midnight, plus or minus an hour." He pushed past me and was gone. Why didn't he say that before?

I decided I'd better not ask that question out loud.

Tessa hung up her phone. "Craig is coming to get us. He told me everything was going to be fine. But how does he know for sure?"

"Everything *is* going to be fine, you'll see."

"Well, you don't know that, Jax, and neither does Craig." Tessa grabbed me by the shoulders. "I didn't kill Misty. You know the money didn't matter."

"I know, Tessa. Don't worry, we'll figure this out."

"And you know I wasn't upset by Rosie's store coming in so close to mine. Right? I didn't try to kill Rosie. Detective Grant is just wrong. He doesn't understand. It's not me." Tessa was in a panic, a state I'd never witnessed her in before.

"Shhhh. It's okay," I said, trying to soothe her. "I know you aren't guilty, but I don't think the detective feels the same way."

"What do you think about Tracy?" Tessa asked. "Tracy must have said something to Detective Grant to make him suspect me."

"She's trying to send him after you to get the focus away from her," I said. "In my mind, it makes her look guilty."

"You've got to help me, Jax."

"We just have to sort through all the junk. You know, like organizing a jumbled box of beads. All we have to do is put each piece in its proper place, and we'll be able to see what we have."

"Well, let's get to work sorting this mess out, before you have to come and visit me in jail."

"Do they allow beads in jail?"

"Probably, but no torches," Tessa said.

"We'll have to solve this mystery ourselves, then, because you can't give up making beads."

NINETEEN

CRAIG SHOWED UP with Joey and Rosie's son Benny. Tessa and I jumped into the SUV, which was infinitely cleaner than Tessa's van. Tessa noticed me admiring it.

"Don't say a word, Jax, I'm already stressed." Once again I had to press my lips shut to keep from saying anything that would get me in trouble.

I had squeezed into the backseat next to two lively four-year-old boys. Joey was holding a small stuffed otter, and Benny had a stuffed seal.

"Hi guys, did you have fun at the aquarium?" Tessa asked from the front seat.

"Yeah, it was neat," said Joey. "We got to see the otters."

"And the seals," Benny chimed in.

"No sharks?" I asked.

"No way, they're too scary!" both boys said together.

Sometimes you don't want to see the scary things, and sometimes you have no choice. Like today. I had looked forward to this weekend for months. Now all I wanted was for this disaster to end, for me to go back to a normal life, and to forget everything I'd experienced in the last day. If I counted the Gumdrop-Mojito debacle and the fact that my cat was still missing, those were yet two more things I wished I could forget, although they could never compare to the horror I'd seen just hours ago.

Craig dropped me off in front of my house, and as soon as I got inside, I collapsed on the sofa. I was glad to be home. I looked around at the terrific place I now called my own. When I'd moved here, I hadn't brought any furniture with me. If it didn't fit in the Ladybug, it didn't make the trip. I'd tried to jazz things up with watercolor paintings of tropical scenes sent to me by my nephew, Jeremy, who at 15 was already an excellent painter. His sunny images didn't quite go with the mish-mash of furniture I had, but it worked for me. The sun-drenched scenes helped keep the place warm and bright even on the coldest, wettest winter days.

I'd refused to accept Val's decorating advice, fearing I'd end up with some animal print accessories if I did. My favorite piece of furniture was an overstuffed chair with faded purple paisley fabric. It was the comfiest chair in the house. I'm sure Aunt Rita spent many hours sitting in this cozy spot. It was Gumdrop's favorite sleeping place. And it was empty.

I took this opportunity to search the house again. I sorted through the laundry, hoping to find him snuggled down inside. I even got out the flashlight and looked under the beds and the sofa.

"Gummie! Here kitty, kitty, kitty," I said, as I swept the flashlight under the bed in the guest room. I had tucked several bead boxes under there. And there was one of Marta's dog collars. Its silver tags flashed as I scanned the carpet. I also realized I needed to vacuum under here more often. There was a serious dust bunny infestation under this bed. I looked under my bed as well, and in all the kitchen cupboards. No Gumdrop. He didn't have any tags on, because he was such a scaredy-cat he never went out. I was careful about keeping the doors shut, but I'd never felt he would make a run for it if I left a door open. How could I have known that a terror named Stanley would put dear Gumdrop in harm's way?

After searching, and searching again, there was simply no way to believe the cat was in the house.

I hoped Animal Control had spotted him and picked him up, or that some kind person, being able to tell he was a loved animal, would turn him over to the pound. I knew it was a long shot to go to Animal Control, but he'd been missing since yesterday morning and this would be the last chance I'd get to check there until Monday. I needed to do something, and this was the only thing I could think to do. I couldn't just wait for Gumdrop to come home. He needed me, and I needed him, too. I put the cat carrier in the Ladybug in the hope that I'd be bringing Gumdrop home with me.

Last time I used this carrier, the two of us were moving to Seattle.

• • •

The day I left Miami, I put the top down on my new VW, slipped Gumdrop into his carrier, and set it in the front seat so he could ride shotgun. He was the most important thing I was bringing with me to Seattle. Jerry wasn't home when I left, and that was fine. I didn't have much to say to him. I left the key to the apartment on the Lino's Pizza menu, and took off.

I drove to my parents' house to say goodbye, and to grab a box of childhood things I couldn't leave behind. Their house was tucked out of the way in the tiny Miami Shores neighborhood, far from the garish Miami Beach hotels and McMansions. I loved this little house on the old street where I grew up. The tile-roofed homes were painted in tropical pastels, and each front yard was shaded with a requisite palm tree or two.

This wasn't going to be a fun conversation.

"Mom, Dad?" I said, as I came in through the front door, the screen door slamming behind me. The house was anything but drab. The living room was a tropical paradise.

"Oh, surely you don't need to go now?" Mom asked, getting up from the sofa's palm frond upholstery and hugging me tightly. "The weather's getting so nice, and it's not hurricane season for a couple more months." Hurricane season was another thing I wouldn't miss.

"Jax, why'd you have to go and say yes to that attorney? You have it so nice here," said my dad.

"You're the one who told me to fish or cut bait, Dad," I said.

"Yes, but we were fishing at the time," he pointed out. It was good advice, no matter what we were doing.

"Well, it's the right thing for me to do." I didn't think it was a good idea to tell them that Gumdrop the psychic cat had told me to move away. Besides, that wouldn't be true, entirely. The one who'd actually told me to go was *me*. Me and Aunt Rita. I liked to think of her as my fairy godmother. Her generous bequeath was pulling me out of my comfort zone so I could live a new life, a better life.

"Why'd Rita say you had to live there in Seattle?" Dad asked, hoisting up his baggy Bermuda shorts. "You've got it so good here in Miami. You've got a job."

"I quit my job, Dad."

A pained expression crossed his face. He rubbed the back of his neck, dark and wrinkled with sun damage from the many years he'd spent fishing.

"Aunt Rita marched to her own drummer, and I respect that," said Mom, defending her aunt. My mother seemed wistful, as if she were considering what it would have been like for her to have chosen a different path.

"Right. And Aunt Rita has helped me hear the drum's beat, and I'm going to march along to it, as well," I said. I loved my parents, but there was no way they could convince me to stay, and no way I could make them understand why I needed to go.

"Gumdrop's out in the car, and I don't want him to overheat. Can you help me with this box?" I turned toward the door, and my parents, with nothing left to say, followed me silently. We walked out the front door, and I showed them the brand-new car. Mom dropped her jaw, and Dad dropped my box.

"You bought a car," they said in unison, breaking their silence.

"Mom. I love you," I said, as I gave her a big hug. "Dad, I love you, too." I gave him a smooch on the cheek. They both stood there on the curb, stunned. I picked up the box, although some of the contents were likely shattered now, and placed it in the trunk. I got behind the wheel, and as I pulled away I looked back at my parents, waving from the curb. I turned the corner, and my cell rang. "Mom" blinked on the screen. Already?

I answered.

"Mom?"

"Don't forget to call me when you get to Seattle."

"I won't forget to call you when I get there." Of course I wouldn't forget.

Gumdrop wasn't a good traveler. He yowled continuously, sounding like Mr. Prescott, Aunt Rita's attorney. "Yelllooooo Yellloooo YEEELLLLLLoooo!" Poor Gumdrop. The vet had given me some kitty Ambien before we left Miami, but I hadn't wanted to give it to him, hoping that once we were on the open road, the smell of fresh air and freedom would calm him down. No such luck. At a rest stop just outside of Orlando I rolled up all the windows, put up the ragtop, and opened the carrier.

"Okay, Gummie, we can do this the hard way, or the extremely difficult way," I said, looking at him. His gray eyebrows furled, (that is, if he had eyebrows), and his eyes were more intense than I'd ever seen them.

He started to howl, "Yellll—" I grabbed him, and then jammed the pill down his throat. I did it so fast he didn't know what happened. He didn't even get a chance to finish his "—llloooo."

Back on the road, Gumdrop fell fast asleep. I felt bad I had to drug the poor guy, but not as bad as I would have felt if I had to listen to his yowling for the next million hours of driving.

The trip to Seattle would take me through 12 of our lovely 50 states. I got on the freeway and kept driving northwest through my home state of Florida, and on and on, finally passing through Idaho and on to Washington State.

It took us four grueling days to get to Seattle. I was on a mission: to begin again, to shake up that old Etch A Sketch called life, and start with a clean slate.

TWENTY

THE ANIMAL CONTROL CENTER was located in a not-so-charming neighborhood that had a hazardous waste disposal depot at one end and a water treatment plant at the other.

"Did any gray cats arrive in the last day?" I asked the woman behind the counter. She'd looked like she was doing some important work on the computer when I came in, her thick glasses pressed close to the screen, her dry red lips pursed in concentration.

"Nope. Sorry, ma'am. Only a kitten and an orange tabby," she said, distractedly, her eyes still on the computer screen. "You're welcome to go and look, if you want. What you see back there is what we got."

I had to see for myself. As I turned the corner to go into the kennel area, I saw what was consuming the clerk's attention: YouTube cat videos. Oh yes, extremely important work. You'd think if she needed to see some cats, she'd walk about 12 feet and see some real live ones who could use the attention, and would probably be doing adorable things, if only given the chance.

The first aisle was filled with rows and rows of cats in cages. Many of them sat still, paws tucked beneath them, staring out through the bars, silent and solemn. Others were asleep, and a few meowed urgently, trying to get anyone's attention. It was excruciating to see all of these missing and unloved cats, and I wished I could adopt them all. I looked in each cage, hoping to see Gumdrop's brilliant green eyes staring out at me. No such luck. He wasn't here.

I turned the corner and walked by the wall of cages that held barking dogs of all sizes and colors. At least a dozen mutts were jumping against the wire cages. I felt sick for the poor dogs that must be scared to death and missing their owners. If Marta were here, she'd correct me and tell me these animals were missing their guardians, not their owners. And then I'd have to punch her in the mouth.

As I passed one cage, I stopped to look at a tiny dark-colored dog with a white stripe across his head that was barking and pawing at the metal doors. He looked like many other dogs here at the pound—except this particular guy looked well cared for and pudgy around the middle. I put my finger up to the cage, and he lunged at it. "RRRRRRRAFFFF!"

"Wait a second. I know you. You're Cheeto, or Tito, or something! What in the world are you doing here?" I said to the furry little monster.

The dog was jumping around wildly at this point, recognizing me, recognizing his name, or maybe just being a small hyper dog. I went out to the front counter to talk with the attendant.

"Do you know anything about the dog in kennel seven?" I asked. "I think he may belong to a friend of mine."

The clerk typed on the keyboard, and a few mouse clicks later, I had an answer. "He was brought in earlier today. Someone dropped him off, said they found him running on the street. No tags." She had pulled back from her screen and squinted at me, trying to refocus her eyes at a distance farther than three inches away.

"I am certain this dog belongs to a friend of mine," I said. "How much will it cost me to spring him from jail?"

"It's $62.50."

I handed her my VISA card. "Sold." At least someone was getting her pet back today.

I jotted my number down on a scrap of paper and handed it to the woman. "Call me if a big fluffy gray cat comes in."

She nodded, and resumed her close inspection of the computer screen, so close her nose was nearly touching the monitor. It was probably a video of a cat playing a piano.

Luckily, I already had Gumdrop's carrier in the car, so I jammed Tito inside, making sure I didn't lose any fingers in the process, and drove straight to Aztec Beads.

TWENTY-ONE

TRACY WASN'T AT HER usual station by the front door when I arrived at Aztec Beads with Tito. Not knowing what else to do, I took him out to the small yard and released him from the carrier. I was glad he decided not to attack me. Instead, he ran off to mark his territory in the dense greenery around the patio.

As I stood under the balcony, I looked up and saw a thin wire hanging down between the floorboards of the deck above me. It looked like the kind of cord that had held Rosie's necklace together. I decided to take a closer look. Maybe this wire or something else on the balcony could give me a clue about what had happened the night before.

There was a jewelry workshop going on in the classroom, and no one was in the shop. Tracy was probably still at the hospital with her mom. The coast was clear. I could go upstairs and take a look around without anyone wondering what I was doing.

I crept up the back stairs and onto the balcony. The thin beading wire was wedged between two planks near the top stair. It didn't look like anyone from the police department had spent any time here looking at this as a crime scene. There was no crime-scene tape or fingerprint dust. That must have meant Detective Grant was still trying to decide if Rosie's near-fatal strangulation was simply an accident that didn't merit an investigation. I looked to see if there were any beads from Rosie's necklace lying around. I didn't spot any, but I did find scrapes on the stairs where Rosie had struggled to get her feet back underneath her.

I decided to be bold and see if I could look around the apartment. Maybe something in there would help me discover whether Tracy was involved in her mother's "accident," and perhaps help me determine if there could be any reason to think Tracy would've wanted Misty dead.

One of the best things would be to discover something that would clear Tessa as a suspect. I tried the sliding glass door, but it was locked. I got a pen out of my handbag and pulled off its cap, then used it to see if I could pop the lock on the door. No such luck. I simply wasn't as competent as MacGyver, from the '80s television show, when it came to improvising tools. If MacGyver were here, he'd have had this door open in about 30 seconds, using only a piece of dental floss and the lint from his pockets. I decided I could at least get the wire out from between the floorboards with the pen's cap, and I knelt down at the bannister to see if I could get it free. I had just grabbed hold of the end of the string and was giving it a good tug when the sliding glass door behind me flew open.

"Get out of here!" It was Tracy, standing in the doorway, her body silhouetted by the lights in the living room behind her. She looked much stronger than I'd seen her before, hands held tightly, elbows bent, like a boxer, ready for a fight.

I jumped up. "Hey, wait, Tracy. It's Jax," I said, trying to calm her.

"Wh—wh—what are you doing here? I thought you were trying to break in. We've had some trouble with that before, people coming up from the alley and trying to unlock the sliding glass door." Had she seen me only seconds before, I would have been one of the people she caught trying to do just that.

"I wanted to check around up here. About your mom's accident."

Tracy was still wound up. "Why would you want to do that, Jax? Coming back to the scene of the crime?"

"No, I dropped off Tito—did you know he was missing?" I said, grasping at anything that might turn her away from the idea that I'd had anything to do with Rosie's injury. "Look, I saw some beading wire stuck between a couple of the boards up here. I wanted to check it out and see if it might be a clue."

"Well, you can stop snooping around and get out of here." Tracy's voice trembled.

"Hey, slow down, I'm not doing anything wrong here. I'm trying to help. I'd like to figure out who hurt your mom."

Tears streaked Tracy's face. "It was you, Jax!" she shouted.

"How could that be?" I said, shocked. "I tried to save your mom. I was right there with you, trying to save her!" I was shouting now, too, so frazzled from the last two days of craziness that I couldn't keep myself pulled together.

"I didn't see anyone with my mom when I first found her choking. You could have pushed her and left her to die," Tracy said. "Then you came back to finish her off." Her shouting decreased as she wiped the tears from her face. Tracy was afraid. I couldn't tell if she was afraid of me, or if it was the thought of losing her mom that frightened her more.

"Tracy, look, I wouldn't do that," I said, forcing myself to relax. My hands were balled into fists, and I opened them, palms out, trying to show her I meant no harm to her or her mother. But she wouldn't let down her guard.

"Jax. Get out!" she demanded. "Just leave before I call the police!"

TWENTY-TWO

I SAT IN THE LADYBUG, my heart pounding. I needed some answers, and there was one person who I knew might be able help—if she was well enough to talk to me. I headed for the hospital. I hated going back after having been there late last night. Hospitals give me the heebie-jeebies.

I hoped Rosie would finally be conscious and could help sort out this mess. If she said she had simply tripped or fallen, then we could all take a big step back and stop pointing fingers at each other about who had tried to murder her. We could instead focus on who killed Misty. Better yet, we could let Detective Grant figure out what happened, and all of us could get back to some semblance of a normal life.

I found Rosie's room and knocked tentatively on the closed door. I nearly jumped out of my skin when a mammoth-sized guy with a beer belly hanging over his belt yanked the door open. He looked like he was expecting someone else.

"Hey, you here to see Leona?"

"Is Rosie here?" I asked in my quiet voice reserved for hospitals and libraries. But, as I heard the ruckus from inside the room, I realized there was absolutely no need to be quiet. There was a slew of people in the room—all apparently visiting Rosie's roommate

Leona. They had spread a hearty picnic across the hospital bed, and everyone was diving into fried chicken and coleslaw. Was that a cooler on the floor?

"That grumpy, bossy woman?" the man asked. "Yeah, she's here, but she's not talkin' so much since they gave her a shot. She'd gotten all up in my face about us bein' so loud."

I could imagine. Rosie was an expert at "up in your face," although I couldn't see how she could have done it while wearing an oxygen mask.

"Well, you guys *are* being a bit noisy," I said, but Leona's friend wasn't paying attention to me anymore. He was opening a giant bag of chips with his teeth and checking to see if he could find a baseball game on the TV.

I sat down next to Rosie's bed. She wasn't moving, but she wasn't asleep, either. If you'd asked me, she looked like she was pretending to sleep. My sister Connie and I used to pretend like that when our mom came to our room and accused us of playing instead of sleeping. I hoped Rosie was just pretending.

"Rosie?"

Silence. All except for Leona's party going on about eight feet away.

Rosie's hands, looking remarkably small, rested on top of the blankets by her sides. I put a hand on top of hers, glad to feel their warmth. I'd never seen her so calm, but right now I'd love to see her yelling at someone, to see she was back to her version of normal.

She had a gauze dressing around her neck, a clear plastic oxygen mask over her face and mouth, and lots of tubes and wires attached to her. Next to the bed, a machine beeped and buzzed, and a read-out showed all sorts of things: heart rate, oxygen levels, temperature, and possibly any recent seismic activity.

Her eyes fluttered and opened. She brought her finger up to her mask and tapped on the side of it. Her lips parted. She was trying to communicate. I pressed the nurse's call button. It was a major miracle when someone came in right away. The nurse looked more like a bouncer than a medical professional, but a bouncer was what we needed at that moment, so it worked out perfectly. The nurse's nametag said Edward. Not Eddie. Not Ed. Edward. Edward was one big, serious dude in aqua scrubs.

"Okay, Leona, time for everyone to go," said the nurse. All of Leona's friends and relatives looked disappointed. Their party was going to have to move. "All of you. Right now. Out of here." Edward was holding the door open for the group of picnickers. Grudgingly, they each picked up something and headed out the door.

"She was pointing to her mouth," I told Edward. "I didn't want to take off her mask without you here."

"Good thinking," the nurse said. "People come in here and think they've seen enough medical shows on TV that they know what they should do, but they don't."

Edward reached down and gently pulled the mask away from Rosie's face.

"Hello there, beautiful," he said with a smile.

In her weak state, she beckoned him closer to her.

"Thanks for getting rid of those assholes," Rosie whispered.

I had trouble keeping a straight face. One thing I knew for sure: Rosie was going to survive. Edward was a true medical pro, and he helped Rosie get comfortable, propped her up in bed, and gave her some juice. He checked her monitors and then left us alone. Leona was still on the other side of the curtain, but since all of her guests had left, the room was absolutely silent except for the machines humming softly.

"Do you feel like talking?" I asked.

Rosie nodded her head.

"I need to tell you I found Tito at the pound today and brought him back to your house." It was probably not the best move I'd ever made, but I wanted Rosie to know it had happened, and that her dog was safe. I thought it was better to tell her about that, rather than mentioning that Tracy had found me lurking on the balcony of her apartment, and was ready to call the cops before I bolted out of there.

Rosie sat up in bed, the wires and tubes straining against her. She looked ready to jump out of bed and go check on Tito to make sure he was fine.

"It's okay. He's happy now that he's home. It sounds like you didn't know he was missing."

"I didn't. Thank you, Jax, for saving him," Rosie said, her voice stronger than I expected. Even so, I could tell it was hard for her to speak.

"Rosie, what I need to know," I said, "is what happened last night. Did someone try to strangle you? Did someone push you down?"

She was quiet for a while before answering. I'm sure she was trying to piece her memories together, as I had tried to do when I was talking with Tessa about what had happened.

"I was standing at the railing, watching the party below, and I was trying to calm down after getting angry with Tracy. I was upset with myself for exploding." Rosie swallowed hard, either from physical pain or from the memory of the fight with her daughter, but probably a little of both. "I heard someone come up from behind. They grabbed my necklace and started to pull it tight around my throat. After that, I'm not so sure what happened. I think someone pushed me, and I remember hitting the stairs hard, or maybe I tripped. I can't remember. It's all a blur."

"Oh, Rosie," I said, now holding her hand with both of mine.

"I was choking, choking, that's all I can remember before everything went dark."

"Do you remember anyone there with you?" I asked.

"You were, Jax, you were there."

"Right, right, I was there helping you get the necklace off and cutting you loose."

"I don't know who else was there. All I remember is you."

"Do you remember Tracy being there?"

"Oh, Tracy *was* there, that's right. I don't remember seeing her. But I could hear her crying and screaming."

I heard a cell phone vibrate. It was on the nightstand between an institutional box of tissue and one of those pink trays shaped like a kidney bean—I have always wondered what those trays were for. Rosie reached for the phone, and I grabbed it, glancing down at the screen as I passed it to her.

Six voicemail messages from a phone number that looked like the one Detective Grant had scribbled on a scrap of paper and handed to me, and had popped up on my phone early today. When Rosie finally talked with him, she'd tell him someone grabbed her necklace and pushed her. And she'd tell him that what she remembered when she was being strangled was that I was there.

Rosie let the call go to voicemail. I only had a short time to sort things out before she talked to the detective.

And then I was going to be in big trouble.

TWENTY-THREE

BACK IN THE LADYBUG, I sat staring out at the rain, big drops plopping on my windshield and skidding down the glass. Good thing I'd remembered to put the convertible's top up.

All Rosie remembered from last night was that I was there. And Tracy, too. I knew I hadn't tried to kill Rosie, but I couldn't be sure about Tracy. It was hard to believe such a sweet young woman would try to harm her own mother, but Tracy's spirit seemed crushed by Rosie's domineering behavior. Could Tracy have snapped and decided to kill her overbearing mother? When I arrived on the balcony last night, I'd found Tracy standing over Rosie. It looked as if she were trying to help her mom, but she just as easily could have been the one who pushed her. Tracy seemed the most likely candidate to kill her mother—she was there at the right time, and she had a reason to commit the crime.

Did Tracy also have a reason to kill Misty? Tracy didn't know Misty, as far as I could tell, so I couldn't think why Tracy would want to kill her. If Tracy killed Misty because her mother had told her to, then I suppose she had a motive. She was at home in the apartment all night, giving her the opportunity. The only thing that didn't make sense was how the same person could commit both of these crimes. If

Tracy was so angry with her mother that she'd tried to kill her, why would she be willing to kill Misty on her mother's behalf? That didn't make sense to me. But murderers were not always the most sensible people. If they were, then I suppose fewer people would end up dead.

There were too many questions, and I needed some answers. I called Tessa.

"Tessa, we've got to talk."

"Where are you?"

"Sitting in my car in the hospital parking lot."

"Well, you better get over to Aztec Beads right away."

I wondered what the newest crisis was.

"Dylan's jewelry workshop starts in 10 minutes."

"Oh, no, I've got to be there to support him."

I drove as fast as I could to the shop, and arrived as Dylan was setting up.

"Hey, Jax. How's it goin'?" said Dylan, in his usual casual tone.

"Great," I lied. "I wanted to make it back in time for your presentation." That part was true.

"Cool. Well, I'm just about to start. I've got these beads that I made. I'm gonna show how to braid these leather strips to make a bracelet. I hope the bead ladies don't think it's too rustic or manly."

"Nonsense," said Tessa, joining us at the front of the classroom. "Rustic is in fashion right now, and besides, we like to be able to make things for the men in our lives now and then." I knew she was fibbing. First, the little Tessa knew about fashion she'd learned from the Lands' End catalog and from watching *Project Runway*. Neither of those sources gave her any authority to judge what was fashionable. And the only two guys I knew she gave gifts to were her husband Craig, who didn't like anything beady, and her son Joey, who liked beads—but mostly to throw instead of rocks.

I noticed one of the leather strips Dylan was using for class had fallen on the floor. As I reached to pick it up, Tito snapped it up and dragged it away. I followed, and found him hiding under a chair in the classroom chewing on his prize. I decided there was plenty of leather to go around, and let Tito keep that piece.

Dylan got started showing the class what to do, and as I watched his demo, all I could think was that Misty had died by being choked with a strap—like the piece of leather Dylan was using in his demo. Why would Dylan want to kill Misty? And if he killed Misty, was there any reason to suspect he would have also tried to kill Rosie? Dylan had met Rosie at the party when I'd introduced them. I remembered they acted strangely when they saw each other. Then again, neither of them seemed to be coping well with the crowded party scene. I couldn't be certain I'd seen anything strange at all.

After Dylan's class, he stood next to his display, speaking with some of the people who were gathering the supplies they needed to complete the bracelet project. Dylan did an impressive job talking about his beads and how he made them. There were several bead ladies standing around him, holding his beads.

"Oh, Dylan, what about this one? It's so light. Is it hollow?" asked a plump woman trying to get his attention, her chandelier-style earrings hanging so low they skimmed her shoulders as she pressed in close to the display.

Another woman, who was wearing a giant dragon necklace made entirely of tiny seed beads, elbowed her way in front of the plump woman, "Dylan, ohhh, do you have any more of these? I love the swirls."

Yet another woman, this one wearing so many bracelets it was a wonder she could move her arms at all, squeezed in close. "Do you think you could make me a matching set like this, but in purple?"

Dylan was experiencing his first bead-buyers' feeding frenzy. A half-dozen women were attempting to nab the best beads before their friends could, all of them trying to get his attention. Dylan, standing a full head taller than the rest of the crowd, was having trouble figuring out which woman he should help first.

"Uh, yes, it's hollow. And, uh, I have one more like that one with the swirls around here somewhere. And, yes, I could make some more like that in purple."

This led to another frenzy of activity in which the bead ladies, all realizing he could create custom orders, started shouting out what they'd like him to make for them. He was quite the salesman, recommending which beads would work best for various projects. Finally, the frenzy died down. In the course of an hour, he sold out of his entire stock of beads, and took orders for more. He seemed delighted with his success.

As Dylan was getting ready to go, Tracy came downstairs and into the gallery. She saw Dylan and stopped in her tracks. They locked eyes for a moment, and then Tracy turned and ran back up the stairs. Dylan returned to his work and said nothing, his head bowed, a grim look on his face. This time I knew I was seeing more than just an awkward moment. This was full-fledged recognition, in which both parties seemed distressed. I was certain of that.

"Dylan, what just happened there?" I asked.

"I tried to tell you at the party, Jax, but I just never had the right moment. And then Rosie got hurt, and I didn't see you again until now."

I stood there, hands on my hips, looking at him silently. Waiting to hear what he had to say.

"Tracy was my girlfriend. I loved her very much. She moved away, and I never heard from her again. The end." Dylan tried to shrug it off, but he was doing a terrible job of convincing me he didn't care.

"Geez! Dylan," I said, ready to scream at him. Actually, I may have been screaming at him. "When was this?"

"About five years ago, when we graduated from high school. We'd been together for a couple of years. She was the love of my life, ya know? Then Rosie dragged her away to Spokane so Tracy could go to college. I'd email her and call her, but she'd never respond. I figured she'd found some new college guy, and didn't want me anymore."

"And Rosie, what did she think of seeing you in her shop?"

"When I saw her at the party, I don't think she recognized me. I thought she looked familiar, and then when you said her name, I figured it out. When Tracy and I were together, I didn't ever go over to their house. I was never sure if that was because Tracy was scared of her mother and didn't want to upset her by bringing me home, or if she didn't want her mom to scare me away."

"But you must have known they had moved back. How could you have *not* known?"

"Look, I lost track of them. Tracy didn't want to be in touch. I had given up and moved on. I'd seen the new bead store, but the application for the show went to that JOWL lady, so I never needed to come in here, you know? The first time I was here was at the party," said Dylan.

I was taking this all in. "Wow, Dylan." All I could say was, "Wow." I certainly hadn't seen this coming. So far, this weekend had been filled with one shock after another.

"Just now, that was the first time I've seen Tracy since we grad-uated from high school." He reached up and scratched the edge of one of his green eyes. It might have been a tear.

"It didn't seem like she was glad to see you."

"No, not at all," he said, sounding heartbroken.

"Oh, Dylan, I'm sorry. You must have been devastated. What happened after she left?"

"I spent a lot of time trying to forget her, trying to feel no pain. In not good ways, you know? It got so bad my parents threw me out. I thought I had gotten over her back then, but I guess not."

And with that, Dylan finished filling his backpack, slung it over his shoulder, and slid out the door.

I found Tessa sitting on the back patio, talking with The Twins.

"Excuse me, Tessa, we need to go and take care of that thing." I was trying to be discreet, to get her away from Sara and Lara with-out spilling the shocking news I'd just received from Dylan.

"Thing? What thing?"

"You know, that important thing we talked about earlier," I said, reaching over and subtly pinching her on the back of the neck.

"Ow! Oh, right, I almost forgot," said Tessa.

We headed out the gate and down the alley, now cleared of the crime-scene tape. A brand-new Dumpster had replaced the one where I had found Misty. All traces of her murder had been erased, except from my memory. We walked to Starbucks and as we did, we filled each other in on what we'd found out.

Tessa went first. "I had a long talk with Sara and Lara. Those two told me how much they hated Rosie."

"Did they say why?" I asked.

"Something about her not respecting their work."

"Yes, that sounds like something they'd say," I said.

"But they don't like anyone, so I don't think they singled out Rosie," concluded Tessa.

"But Tessa, listen to this." I told her what I had just witnessed with Dylan and Tracy.

"You have got to be kidding me." We stopped in the alley. Tessa was stunned, and it didn't seem like she could walk and think at the same time. I pulled her along. I was on a mission: coffee.

"Tessa, can you go back and talk with Tracy about the Dylan situation?"

"Me? What about you?"

"Well, Tracy is angry with me right now. She kind of caught me on her balcony, snooping around."

"What?"

"You see, I was out in the backyard and I saw this piece of beading wire on the underside of the balcony, and I went up to check it out. You know, looking for clues to help my best friend not get arrested for murder."

"Good."

"But while I was there, Tracy came home and caught me. She thought I was returning to the scene of the crime."

"Bad."

"So that's when I went to the hospital to see Rosie."

"Good."

"Except Rosie thinks I strangled her. I know. You don't have to say it. 'Bad!'"

"Doesn't Tracy think *I* tried to kill her mom?" Tessa asked. "It seems like that's what she told Detective Grant."

"I'm not sure what Tracy is thinking now, especially having just seen Dylan. Can you please talk with her?" I gave Tessa my most pathetic, pleading grimace.

"Okay, but you owe me one."

By now, we'd gotten to the coffee shop, and I'd ordered a grande latte for myself and a shot of espresso for Tessa. How that woman could survive on so little caffeine amazed me.

"Notice I'm buying your drink, Tessa."

"That's not enough. When this whole thing is over, I want you to buy me several proper drinks. You know, the kind with alcohol in them."

"Absolutely, Tessa. I'll have a few, too."

We walked back to Aztec Beads in silence. Tessa and I needed to put each of the facts together one by one, like beads on a strand. And we needed to find the bits that were missing so we could finish our project—a project we didn't choose, but one we needed to complete.

Tessa headed up the outside staircase, giving me a long backward glance as she went.

I closed the gate to the patio and was struck with the vision of Dylan walking in through this gate last night at the party. Dylan had been in the alley around the time Misty was murdered. I had no idea what it meant, if anything, but it certainly didn't look good for Dylan, because there was absolutely no reason for him to have been in the alley, other than what was likely the truth: He simply wanted to sneak in and avoid the crush of people.

I wandered into the classroom to see what was happening. My poor brain was on overload, and I thought it might be fun to see part of a class, since I'd not seen much so far.

"And now we have Marta and her dog collars," Judy announced from the front of the room. She applauded, and Marta began her presentation.

I stood in the back of the room, leaning against the wall.

"Hello there, Jax. I'm relieved to see you survived last night," Allen said as he sidled up close to me, and gave me a warm smile. I was glad he was being so friendly, and that my heroics from last night hadn't scared him away. Maybe that quick view of my Spanx was enough to make him want to see more, although I seriously doubted it. I turned and smiled at him. He was a bit of sunshine in my otherwise cruddy day. I wanted to talk with him, but Marta was getting started, so we had to keep quiet.

"First of all, for our very, very special friends, we do not call them dog collars," Marta said, giving Judy a cold glance. "That is just so insulting. I prefer 'dog jewelry.'"

Allen and I looked at each other skeptically.

"Our most popular items are dog necklaces. Some doggies will wear bracelets. But we find they just want to chew them off."

"I would," Allen whispered.

I tried not to laugh as Marta continued.

"We are also looking into a line of microchip piercings for an edgier look."

Allen raised his hand. "Can you explain what that means?" I couldn't tell if he was having fun, or genuinely wanted to know what she was talking about.

"You know how you can get a little microchip put under a dog's skin so the owner can be located if the dog gets lost?" Marta said, "I'm working with a vet so we can make a fashion statement out of those microchips. The little piece of silicon can be embedded into a pierced earring with a flashy rhinestone on it."

"Or, maybe a metal stud for the butch dogs, like a Doberman," Allen suggested, playing along.

"Exactly," Marta said. I had to turn away and pretend to cough so I didn't break out laughing.

"We are also developing a line of tail decorations."

"Doesn't that get too close, you know, to the bodily functions?" I asked, as appropriately as possible.

"Yes, well, that has been a challenge, and we are still working on it. That's why, for now, I'm focused on the necklaces. For today's demonstration, I'll be showing you how to make a cute little charm for your dog to wear around his or her neck."

Marta proceeded to show us how to use wire to make a charm by stacking a series of beads together and then making a loop at the top.

"And you're done. Easy, right?" Marta said, and the audience clapped politely.

As others had done, Marta spent some time after her workshop talking with potential customers at the front of the classroom. "My basic necklace design has a series of four glass beads, two on each side of the identification tag. I have several different designs to choose from: paw prints, flowers, bones, and hearts. Each of these is sewn to a high-quality fabric ribbon. Then, I add other adornments to the necklace, like pressed beads from the Czech Republic, Japanese seed beads, and semi-precious stones."

"How much does one of these 'necklaces' cost?" Allen asked.

"The custom orders cost 275 dollars. And the 'off the shelf' version that contains one of each of the handmade bead designs is a bargain at 175 dollars," Marta said.

"A bargain," I whispered into Allen's ear.

"Do you have any idea how many minutes that collar would last on my black lab?" Allen asked me in a whisper.

"Ten minutes?"

"Max."

"In addition to the dog jewelry," Marta continued, "I make individual beads of many of the most popular dog breeds. I've got a sample of some of them on my display pedestal. They're only 100 dollars, and for an additional fee, I can customize the bead to look like your own animal companion," said Marta, with a broad smile.

We wandered over to look at the glass dog beads. They didn't look good. All of them were too melted and droopy, like they had been in a hot torch for too long.

"I think she should stick to the dogs with lots of wrinkles, you know, all the hounds, shar-peis, maybe some bulldogs," I whispered, examining what was supposed to be a chocolate lab, but looked more like a Hershey's Kiss.

"Maybe she just needs some lessons from you," Allen said, as he looked over my shoulder at the beads.

"Oh, flattery will not get you anywhere." Although what I was really thinking was that flattery could actually get him almost anywhere with me.

"Damn, I thought that might work," Allen said, giving my shoulders a soft squeeze.

Marta came hustling over to me. "Oh, Jax, some doggie-lovers want to take me out to dinner, so I won't be home for a while."

"What about Stanley?"

"Oh, he'll be fine. Just take him out once or twice to do his you-know-what. Okay?"

"I don't know if I can—"

"Oh, super! Jax, thanks."

I watched through the front window of the shop as Marta toddled off toward her SUV with a couple of bead ladies.

"How are you feeling after last night? How is Rosie?" Allen asked.

"Rosie is still in the hospital and recovering, but I'm a wreck. Did you hear about the young beadmaker, Misty?"

"I want to hear all the updates. Seems like a great deal has happened since I saw you speed away in the ambulance last night." That was an understatement.

"How about I invite myself over and cook you dinner?" Allen asked.

"That would be fantastic," I said. I'd never had a guy make food for me. Jerry ordering pizza, slicing it, and putting it on a paper plate didn't qualify as cooking, in my mind.

"You go home and relax, and I'll come by later with some groceries. Do you need a lift?"

"No, I've got my car. See you around seven?"

It felt great to have a man want to hear about my day and to feed me. I could get used to that.

TWENTY-FOUR

ONCE I GOT HOME, I stripped off my clothes, and was tempted to throw them away like I had the night before. Instead, I aimed them at the hamper. If I kept throwing my clothing away after every traumatic event, I'd soon have nothing left to wear.

I showered, gave my hair the world's fastest blow-dry, and once again was faced with the dilemma of what to wear. Should I wear something fancy? That was probably not the best thing, since Allen was just coming over to make dinner. If I wore what I usually did when I was hanging around at home, he'd be pretty unimpressed: my oldest jeans and an oversized floppy T-shirt. I put on some cute black stretchy pants. Some people call them yoga pants. However, since I'd never done yoga in them, and had no plans to do yoga in them, I think that would be rather misleading. I added a silky purple top—long enough to cover my backside without looking frumpy—and, of course, a fabulous necklace. I chose a long silver chain with a pendant. It was deep purple and covered with dots, each one looking like a small bull's-eye.

A few minutes before seven, I headed down the hall, passing the guest room. I could hear Stanley snoring inside. I lay down on the sofa to rest my eyes. It had been a long couple of days, with not enough sleep.

When the doorbell rang, I jumped up, startled. This had been a weekend of being wrenched from sleep by the doorbell. I tried to smooth myself out before I answered it.

"Pike Place Market—I never get tired of going there." Allen dropped his leather messenger bag on the floor by one of my kitchen table's big claw-footed legs, then plopped two bags on the counter containing the ingredients for our dinner. "I love all the beautiful displays of fruits and vegetables. The fish-sellers throwing salmon around. Oh, and the flowers," Allen said, as he whipped out a beautiful bouquet of vibrant spring flowers from of one of the bags. "I thought you could use something to cheer you up after a difficult couple of days."

"Oh, thank you, Allen," I said giving, him half a hug. He smelled good, like spearmint. In a good way, not in the "crazy woman's cat dumped catnip-laced mojito on me" way. I retreated to the china hutch to see if I could find a vase for the flowers. I was glad I'd turned away from Allen, because I was feeling flushed at that moment.

Just relax and have fun, I reminded myself.

That's what Val would say. She'd say more than that, but I told that little voice inside my head to behave itself. I wished my kitchen was nicer than it was, with its funky old cabinets more suited for a garage than someone's home. I'd tried to jazz up the kitchen with a glass mosaic backsplash, but glass will only go so far in turning a sow's ear into a silk purse. The image of a pig wearing fancy earrings made of sparkling beads made me smile, and then, finally, I was able to relax and turn back to Allen, with the flowers now in an iridescent art glass vase.

He pulled out an expensive bottle of zinfandel from one of the bags. "Finally, we get to have our bottle of wine." He opened the drawer next to my fridge and pulled out the opener. I looked at him quizzically. It was hard to believe he was feeling so at home in my kitchen, and that he, like Gumdrop, had psychic powers.

"I made drinks in this kitchen a couple of nights ago, remember? I found the wine opener right next to the muddler."

"The muddler you used to mash the catnip?" I asked, trying to smile after such a catastrophe. He must have recovered, because he was here at my house once again. I was glad we could joke about it.

"And your cat, is he going to come and attack me for some random reason tonight?"

"Gumdrop disappeared. He either ran away or is an expert at hiding. I'm not sure which."

"I hope he wasn't traumatized after his frenzy with me, or should I say *on* me."

"I'm almost positive it was because a dog moved in for the weekend and, well, Gumdrop doesn't like dogs."

I found two wineglasses that actually matched and had no chips in them, and poured the wine.

"To Gumdrop, and his safe return," toasted Allen.

"To Gummie, I miss you." We clinked glasses as Allen stepped closer to me, looking over the top of his drink with a smile. He stopped to admire the pendant I was wearing. He picked up the bead from my chest, pausing just a little longer than I was comfortable with, to examine the piece closely. I tried to look calm, but inside I was hyperventilating. I was definitely out of practice with this dating thing, so I broke away before I grabbed him, which I didn't think would be an appropriate move so early in the evening.

"Sooooo, let's get dinner started," I said, moving past him. "This is an ancient AGA stove. It's tricky to use but just too lovely to get rid of." Aunt Rita's old stove was a cheerful yellow enamel, and solid as a rock. I had planned to learn to cook well enough that I'd be able to do more with my oven than bake a potato, although I'd not made much progress so far. I hoped, as well, that someday I'd be able to remodel the whole kitchen around this stove. For now, all I could afford was a new coat of paint, provided that Rudy stopped watching old sci-fi movies with Val long enough to give me a quote.

Allen made a delicious dinner: a lovely piece of sautéed salmon with dill and lemon sauce, a crisp green salad, a crunchy loaf of bread, and a tiny box of truffles for dessert.

We brought the last of the wine and the truffles over to the sofa.

"Do you want a truffle?" Allen asked. What a silly question. I'd never said no to chocolate in my whole life.

"Absolutely."

From a golden box, Allen extracted a truffle, covered delicately with cocoa powder.

"Open your mouth."

Oh, dear. He was going to feed me a truffle. I couldn't say no, so I acquiesced, trying to chew as sexily as possible. I waited until I'd swallowed before I spoke, as my mother had taught me.

"Delicious," I said, and just as the words came out of my mouth, he reached right over and kissed me. I hadn't expected that.

"Oh yes, very delicious," Allen agreed, pulling me close. "Want another?" I wasn't sure if he was asking if I wanted another truffle or another kiss.

"No, I'm fine; I'll have another a little later." I could have said yes. Why didn't I say yes?

"Show me the beads you made the other night," Allen requested, changing gears and standing, knowing he'd been rebuffed, although I hadn't meant it.

"Oh, right, I haven't looked at them yet," I said, changing direction right along with him. "It always delights me to see how my beads have turned out when I pull them out of the kiln. There are always surprises, usually good ones."

I spotted Allen's messenger bag under the table as we got up to go to the studio. I thought we'd better not leave it unattended, in case Stanley woke up and decided it looked like a good snack.

"I'll just pick this up," I said reaching under the table and fumbling for the strap. "We've got a dog staying here right now who likes to chew on fine leather goods."

As I reached for Allen's satchel, he ran over to take it from me. As I lifted it, the strap caught on the bottom of the bag, and its contents came spilling out. Several large glass beads scattered across the hardwood floor.

They were beads from many different beadmakers—the beautiful pieces from Rosie's special necklace, and several of my beads too.

"Where did you get these beads?" I demanded.

Immediately Allen was down on his hands and knees. "It's not what it looks like," he said, frantically picking up the beads, and scooping them back into his bag.

"I don't know what it looks like to you, Allen, but to me it looks like someone has been stealing beads." I yanked at the strap of his bag.

"It's not like that. I can assure you," he said.

"And these beads of mine—they're from the bracelet I had on at the party."

"I can explain."

"Let's hear it," I said, standing over him.

"I found the beads when I was cleaning up after the ambulance left," Allen said. "I was trying to take care of them, to keep them safe."

"Why didn't you tell someone you had them?"

"I didn't think they mattered. I thought I'd hold onto them until Rosie was out of the hospital."

"They're needed for a police investigation."

"Police investigation? Because of Rosie's accident?"

"The detective thinks what happened to Rosie might not have been an accident," I said.

"Really, Jax, I had no idea," Allen said. "Don't you believe me?"

"I can't figure out why you wouldn't have given the beads to someone at the bead shop. You could have left them there today."

I thought about what Detective Grant had said. The beads were evidence he needed in order to find the person who strangled Rosie. Could Allen have stolen the beads to hide evidence?

"Are you trying to protect someone by keeping these beads from the police? Or, maybe you're the one trying to avoid being impli-cated in Rosie's attempted murder."

"Jax, that's just crazy. Why would I want to kill Rosie? I don't even know her." Allen stood up, gripping his bag's strap tightly.

"Leave the beads here. I have officially confiscated them. I'll be calling Detective Grant in the morning to let him know you've been found with crucial evidence."

He scooped the beads out of his messenger bag and put them on the table, leaving several lying on the floor. He slung the bag onto his shoulder, and walked out the door, not looking back.

I carefully placed all of the beads in a Ziploc bag and left them on the coffee table. I wanted them to be safe until I could call the detective in the morning.

Did Allen have any reason to hide evidence? Could he have something to do with the attack on Rosie? Or Misty's murder? Was Allen just a thief? Or a murderer?

Seconds later, there was a knock on the front door.

"Look, Allen—," but it wasn't Allen. It was Val.

"Geez, Val. Get in here," I said, ushering her in.

"I see you were entertaining a man here tonight." Entertaining made it sound like I had my tap shoes on, and was singing a show tune.

"Yes, I was," I said, noticing my jaw was clenched tight. I tried to loosen it by rubbing my cheek and opening my mouth a little.

"But I'm confused. He just left, and you slammed the door. And, it's only ten o'clock. That's not usually how these evenings end," Val said.

"That's not how they end for *you*, Val. For me, that's how this one ends." Pretty much every other date I've had recently has ended in a catastrophic way.

"Oh, darling," Val said, "I'm so sorry." She gave me a big hug that nearly crushed me. That girl didn't know her own strength.

"I caught him stealing. He had beads from Rosie's necklace, and a bunch of my beads, too."

"Oh goodness, honey, I didn't think guys stooped so low as to steal beads. Did he explain himself?"

"He tried to, but I'm not sure I believed him."

"Let's just relax and finish this wine," Val said, picking up the bottle. "Oh, zinfandel, my favorite." Every kind of wine was Val's favorite, especially when she didn't have to pay for it. "Ohhhh, and truffles! We'll bring those with us, too."

"Do you mind if we sit out back?" I asked. "I need to cool down."

Val and I walked through the house and out to the patio behind my studio. We sat at the little bistro table, wrapped in the fleece blankets I kept near the backdoor to use on chilly Seattle nights like this one. "Cheers!" I said, once we'd gotten settled.

"Back at 'cha," said Val, taking a sip and settling into her chair.

When the wine was gone, Val went home, as usual. I crawled into bed but couldn't sleep. I didn't have Gumdrop to snuggle with. I remembered I needed to check my email and see if anyone had responded to the Craigslist posting about Gumdrop. I grabbed my laptop and flopped back onto the bed. As long as Marta was visiting, I didn't have my office to work in, so my bed would have to do. I logged in. I didn't have any mail, except for spam offering to increase my penis size (unlikely) and another message requesting me to send large sums of money to an African country (unwise).

As I sat there looking at the laptop screen, I thought about Andy. My geeky brother Andy. He'd gone to school at the University of Miami and gotten a degree in computer science in just three years. Then he'd gone out to California to get a Ph.D., ratcheting his level of genius a step higher. These days, he was the founder of a randomly named software company called Pook that specialized in cyber-security. The best thing about having a family member who works in the Internet security business is that they can do hi-tech snooping for you.

I called him up.

"Hey, little brother. How are you?"

"Yeah. Hey, Jax." He sounded groggy.

"I hope I'm not calling too late."

"Oh, no, Jax, it's okay. I'm doing some late-night coding for a new software release we have coming up. I must've fallen asleep on the keyboard, judging from the million letter Y's typed across the screen and the keyboard-shaped dent on my forehead."

This wasn't the first time I had called Andy late at night and found him working.

"I have a favor to ask. Can you check up on a guy named Allen Sinclair? I have some suspicions about him, and I'm trying to figure out if I should trust him." There was a long pause on the other end of the phone. "Bro?"

"Oh, yeah, sorry, I'm still dazed. Go ahead."

"He lives in Seattle, mid-40s, works at the *Seattle Times*. I don't have much to go on other than that."

"What kind of crimes are we talking about?"

"He's a jewelry thief."

"You mean like diamonds and rubies?"

"Glass beads. But they're still precious."

Andy seemed disappointed to hear we weren't talking about a heist of millions of dollars in gems.

"Or, it is possible he's a murderer," I added.

"Now, that would be more exciting than someone who steals beads," Andy said. "Let me do some checking and see what I can find out. Too bad he has such a common name; that'll make it harder to find him. Oh, and Jax, you might not want to mention this to anyone, because some of this, strictly speaking, falls outside of what is considered legal."

"Got it. Oh, and call Dad. The last time I talked with him, he said you never call."

"One favor at a time, Sis, one favor at a time."

I laughed and hung up the phone, hoping he was as much a wizard at digital breaking-and-entering as he claimed. And now, finally, I could sleep.

TWENTY-FIVE

I WAS JOLTED AWAKE by the phone. Tessa's name blinked on the screen as it rang and rang.

"Tessa, I'll call you in the morning," I said sleepily into my pillow, not answering the phone. Then it stopped ringing. And then my phone started ringing again. This time I answered.

"Tessa?"

"Jax! We can't find Izzy. She said she'd be home at ten o'clock."

"What time is it?" I said squinting at the alarm clock. Its red numbers glowed: 10:45. I hadn't been asleep for more than a half-hour. "Why didn't you call her and tell her to get her butt home?"

"I've called her a million times. She's not answering." I could hear the panic in Tessa's voice.

"Don't you have a fancy GPS thing in your minivan?"

"I do, and for the last hour the dot on the map in the program shows the van hasn't moved."

"That's good news, right? You know where Izzy is." That wasn't entirely true. We knew the location of the van, but we didn't know if her daughter was with the van or not. Next time, Tessa was going to have to strap a GPS unit directly onto her teenage daughter.

"Why isn't she answering her phone? If she'd just answer, then I could get some rest, knowing she was okay, or I could rescue her if she needed help."

Finally, I was awake enough to think about this clearly. "Tessa? You confiscated Izzy's phone. It's locked in a drawer at your studio."

"*Che casino! Dio mio!*" Tessa had slipped into Italian. It was a side-effect of all the years she'd spent in Italy after she graduated from high school.

"What's 'casino'? 'Dio' what? Tessa! Speak English!"

"Oh, Jax, this is a mess. What are we going to do?"

"Let's focus here," I said in my calmest voice, although on the inside I was panicking nearly as much as Tessa was. "Where does the GPS say Izzy is?"

"Next to Schmitz Park."

"Where's Craig?" I asked.

"He's on his way out to the park to see if he can find her."

"And he left you at home?" I asked, puzzled that she wouldn't have gone with Craig.

"It seemed like I should stay home in case she showed up here."

"It seems to *me* that the more people who are looking for her, the better. Besides, if she shows up at home, Ashley can call you. You haven't lost her, right?"

"No, you're right. Why didn't I go with Craig? *Mama mia—*"

"Tessa. Tessa?" I urged her to listen before she slipped into Italian again. "Hold on a minute. I'm going to come and get you. We'll go and look for her. It's better for more people to search—more people to cover more ground."

As I talked with her, I hopped on one foot and then the other, juggling the phone as I pulled on jeans and sneakers. I grabbed my purse and a sweatshirt and jumped into the Ladybug. The sky was clear, and I put the top down, hoping the chilly Seattle night would keep me awake, although with the amount of adrenaline coursing through me, I probably didn't need to. I sped toward Tessa's house.

As I drove, I couldn't stop thinking about the delicate wrist with the tiny tattoo I'd seen in the Dumpster earlier today. Misty was someone's daughter, and she was dead. That couldn't be undone. I pushed away the thoughts of Izzy in danger. Izzy was going to be fine.

Tessa was waiting on the curb for me, wrapped in a heavy sweater, her arms crossed to keep out the night's chill. She got in my car, and we sped off to find Izzy.

Schmitz Park was a rambling recreation area close to downtown Seattle. While it wasn't wilderness, it did have enough trails and secluded areas to make it an unsafe place for a girl to be late at night.

"Maybe the minivan broke down. She'd just flag someone down for help." As soon as I said it, I realized I shouldn't have.

"Oh, yes, some homicidal maniac would pull over to help her." Tessa's voice cracked as she started rummaging through her purse, looking for something. "Or worse!"

"Worse? What could be worse than a homicidal maniac?" I asked, but again, I realized I was leading this conversation in the wrong direction.

Tessa pulled out her phone. "I can look at the tracking device on the van and see where she is." Tessa was tapping on the phone's screen. "Here's the map; let me just zoom in. Okay, see the blue dot that's flashing? That's where the van has been for the last hour."

I hated to be the one who kept making things worse, but I needed Tessa to think about what we knew, and what we didn't know. "Tessa, we know where the minivan is, not where Izzy is. She could be with it, or she could have left the van."

"What do you mean 'left the van?" Tessa was nearly hysterical, grabbing the collar of my sweatshirt and pulling me close, as if the closer I was, the clearer I'd be.

"I'm thinking maybe she just stopped for, I don't know, a burger," I said, back-pedaling from a scarier scenario, and pulling myself away from her so I could drive safely.

"At 10:45 at night?" she asked.

"I don't know. All I'm saying is there could be a completely reasonable explanation for what has happened to Izzy." I was grasping at straws. I had no idea where Izzy was, or what she was doing. All I knew was at this moment, she wasn't where she was supposed to be.

"If this is some crazy thing Izzy decided to do for fun, she will be grounded for the rest of her life."

I didn't doubt it.

As I sped along toward the park, I thought about Tessa and me, best friends for as long as I could remember.

• • •

I had called Tessa as soon as I'd made my decision to move to Seattle. She'd moved there after returning from several years in Italy, newly married to Craig, the most non-Italian guy I'd ever met. And she'd met him in Italy. He'd been an intern at the American Embassy when they met, and the rest was history.

"Tessa, you'll never believe it. I'm moving to Seattle."

"That would be terrific, Jax," she said, nearly shouting. "That would be absolutely amazing."

"You remember my great-aunt Rita?" I asked.

"Of course, she made all of those gorgeous quilts," Tessa said.

"When she passed away, I inherited her house."

"Where is it?" Tessa asked.

"I haven't seen the house, and I'm curious about it. Apparently it's located in the Queen Anne district. What do you think? Is that a scummy neighborhood?"

"No, Jax, it's a terrific area."

"Can you drive by and check it out? I want to make sure it isn't a burned-out building. I don't want to give up my entire life here in Miami to move to the other side of the country and live in a fall-ing-down shack." I'd already told Mr. Prescott I was coming, but I could back out if the house was truly uninhabitable. Then the lawyer would sell it, and donate the money to charity. And I'd be stuck in Miami. I hoped Tessa would call me back with good news.

"Sure. What's the address?"

Tessa called back 45 minutes later. She must have left immediately after our phone call, and sped over there and back. She was a notoriously fast driver, and between that and her disaster of a van, she was hell on wheels.

"Jax, the house is the most gorgeous thing ever. It's a giant Craftsman house."

"A bungalow?"

"Way bigger than a bungalow, more like a BIG-galow. It has two doors right at the front. It looks like it's two units."

"That's right, Aunt Rita made it into a duplex."

"Well your Aunt Rita was a genius. The place needs some work, but it has weathered shingles, with a deep burgundy trim. It has a long driveway on one side, and a small garden in front."

"Weathered shingles and burgundy trim sound promising. So does a garden."

"It needs some TLC, but you're the woman to do it."

"As long as I can do the work a little at a time, and can live in it right away, I can do it. It has a roof, right?"

"Yes, silly, it has a roof. So? You're coming? You're sure?" Tessa asked.

"I am. Give me a week, and I'll be there."

● ● ●

Tessa called Craig to tell him we were on our way to the park to help search for Izzy. He tried to discourage us from coming, but Craig and I both knew there was no stopping Tessa.

Tessa had her eyes glued to the tiny screen with the blue dot. It was her only connection to her daughter at that moment. I wasn't sure whether she wanted to see the blinking spot moving or not, but I knew she was thinking all sorts of terrible thoughts, and only finding her girl was going to make things better.

We parked on a residential street next to the park, and I grabbed my flashlight from the Ladybug's trunk. Tessa and I walked up the wide trail into the darkness. Up ahead we saw the outline of the van, and when Tessa spotted it, she started running toward it. I could hear Craig's voice calling for us, but I couldn't see him. When I finally reached the van, we saw Craig—and Izzy was with him. They appeared at the top of a hill, coming down a long path flanked by redwoods. Tessa leaned against the side of the van and started sobbing in relief, releasing all of the tension she'd been holding in. Izzy ran ahead of her dad and collapsed into her mother's arms, pressing her face against Tessa's chest.

"Mom, I'm so sorry. I was looking for this awesome party some friends were having at Alki Beach, and I got lost. I didn't have my phone so I couldn't figure out where I was."

"But what about the map in the glove compartment?" Tessa asked, pulling her daughter back to look her in the eye.

"I thought there were just gloves in the glove compartment." Oh, Izzy, she had so many things to learn. "And then I ran out of gas..."

"Because you didn't use the money I gave you yesterday to fill up the tank."

"I just kinda forgot," Izzy sobbed. "I'm sorry. I will be the best daughter ever for the rest of my life if you'll just understand I didn't mean to do this."

Craig had reached us, taken off his coat, and wrapped it around Izzy, who was dressed in only a light sweater and jeans. It was a way he could protect her, even if only for a short time. Izzy was growing up, and she'd be spending more time away from home in the next few years. I hoped she wouldn't have too many scary adventures like this. I didn't want to keep rescuing Tessa, and her daughter, in the middle of the night.

"Why didn't you go to a house in this neighborhood and ask for help?" Craig asked.

"The houses were all dark. It was too spooky." The logic of a 16-year-old girl was hard to understand. "So I saw a sign for Alki, and I thought if I could just get to my friends, they could help me with the car."

"You headed off into the darkness to find your friends?" Tessa asked, trying to clarify the completely illogical thought process Izzy had used.

"Yes, Mommy, I'm so sorry," Izzy said. I noted her use of the word "Mommy." This was Izzy's way of being endearing. I'm sure she hoped to avoid any unpleasant punishment by being as adorable as possible.

"Let's all get home, okay?" said Craig. "We'll leave the van here and get some gas for it tomorrow."

Izzy opted to go with her dad, figuring, I supposed, it was safer to go home with him than face the intense questioning that would have occurred if she'd come back with Tessa and me.

"She is grounded for life, but I am so glad we found her before anything terrible happened," Tessa said. "When I saw her running toward us, I was happy and angry at the same time. I wanted to spank her and hug her."

"Don't you think she's too old to spank? And isn't spanking a bad thing these days?"

"Yes on both counts, but I am allowed to feel it, even if I don't actually do it, right?"

I wasn't a mother myself, but I certainly had the desire to spank my current houseguest and her dog. Clearly, I was starting to lose my mind from lack of sleep as I fantasized about putting both of them over my knee. I decided it was time to change the topic, before I had any more sleep-deprived imagery in my brain. "I guess Izzy now knows you have a tracking device in your van."

"She hasn't quite figured that out. She just thinks we magically appeared, as parents are supposed to do when their children are in trouble."

"She'll figure it out once she calms down," I told her, "and then you're busted."

"Tracy filled me in on all sorts of interesting things today," said Tessa, moving on to the next important crisis now that Izzy was safe and sound.

"What did you learn about Tracy and Dylan?" I asked.

"Rosie didn't want her daughter to be with Dylan, so she took Tracy away to Spokane to go to Eastern Washington University. According to Tracy, Rosie told her to never be in touch with Dylan again."

"But why? Why did she want to keep them apart? I don't get it."

"Rosie thought Dylan was a bad influence," said Tessa.

"Did Tracy say what would have happened if she had been in touch with Dylan after they moved away?"

"She said Rosie would have thrown her out, and she'd no longer support her or help her get through college. She stopped talking after that. Of course, I knew what choice she'd made."

"Did she say why she ran away when she saw Dylan?" I asked.

"I think she was overwhelmed, and ashamed she'd left him behind years ago."

"What a choice—someone she loved, or getting an education. Tracy must have hated her mother for that," I said.

"I think so," Tessa agreed. "As much as she hated her mother for forcing her to leave Dylan, and with how badly Rosie treated her daughter every day, I have to wonder if Tracy really did try to kill Rosie."

"Don't you think if Tracy was the killer, she'd have said something different to you? Like everything was fine, and she was happy with the choice she'd made? If she'd said that, then she'd be saying she had no reason to kill her mom."

"In other words," Tessa said, "Tracy is telling the truth. And that means she's *not* the killer. Or Tracy is lying, and that means she *is* the killer."

"It means she *could* be the killer, not *is* the killer," I explained. "But, Tessa, think about it. Tracy is not the only one who hates Rosie for taking her daughter away."

"Oh, Jax, don't tell me Dylan could have tried to kill Rosie. I feel like he's an extra child of mine. I trust him to run the studio and to be around my kids."

Tessa was searching around in my car for a tissue. She found an unused napkin and blotted her eyes. The combination of Izzy's disappearance and the revelations about Dylan were too much for her to handle.

We drove for a while in silence. Ideas rattled around in my head, but it was hard to grasp one of them before it went bouncing away.

"Tessa? Do you know where we can find Nick right now?"

"He's probably down on The Ave." For some reason, the street called University Way near the University of Washington campus was nicknamed "The Ave" and not "The Way."

"Let's go," I said.

"What? Seriously? It's not the best place to go at night, especially for two middle-aged women in a red VW."

"Nick can tell us more about Misty," I said. "We don't know much about her. Maybe he can tell us how things were between her and Dylan. Nick's known Dylan for a long time. Maybe he can also tell us what happened after Tracy left."

Tessa sighed, wiped her cheek, and tossed the napkin on the floor. If she hadn't been so upset, I'd have told her to put it in her purse and throw it away later. I didn't want the Ladybug to end up looking like her van.

"We'll be careful," I promised. Tessa sighed again.

"I can take you home before I go," I offered.

"Oh, no, Jax, there's no way I'm letting you drive around all by yourself on The Ave in the middle of the night."

TWENTY-SIX

WE DROVE UP AND DOWN The Ave, scanning the faces of young people standing around in knots, leaning against walls, sitting on blankets with their dogs, and playing guitars. These kids, barely adults, were smoking, drinking, and talking loudly. At night, this was their place, their community.

There were college students out on The Ave, too, but they tended to inhabit the street during the day, and at night they all seemed to be headed somewhere in groups, moving down the street toward a destination, not just hanging around.

"Can't you just call Nick?" I asked.

"He doesn't have a phone."

"Right. I knew that."

People stared at us as we drove by, and we got a few whistles, but I think they were for the Ladybug and not us. Tessa was old enough to be the mother of some of these kids. I suppose that made me old enough to be a parent, as well, but I didn't want to think about it.

We stopped at a red light, and I heard an engine rev next to me. I turned to see a hefty guy on a Harley, his black helmet gleaming in the streetlight, a long beard hanging down over his leather vest. He gave me a nod. "Nice ride," he said, and he revved his engine again. The light turned green and the guy took off. I started to accelerate.

"No racing, okay?" Tessa commanded, grabbing my hand as I reached for the stick shift.

"Oh, me? No, I wouldn't do that." It was a good thing she'd warned me, because I would have tried to beat that guy to the next light, given the opportunity.

We drove down The Ave and then turned around and came back up toward 45th. We spotted Nick standing outside a dive bar, with a couple of other guys.

"Nick! Nick!" I yelled as I pulled to the curb. He'd seen us and moved quickly toward my car.

"Hey, Tessa, Jax," said Nick, as he crouched next to our car. He smelled like a bad combination of Rainier Beer and smoke. "You guys should probably not be out here this late at night."

"Yes, we noticed that," I said with a nervous smile.

"We need to talk with you." I could hear the strain in Tessa's voice.

"Can't it wait until tomorrow, Tessa? I'll come by Fremont Fire, and we can talk all you want," Nick said, teetering on his heels and falling backward before catching himself.

"We're trying to find out more about Misty," I said. "We think you might be able to help us." I didn't like being stopped here and was worried we might be carjacked at any moment.

"Look, Misty's gone," he muttered. "I'm trying to forget about her, you know, hoping to get wasted and stop feeling anything for a while."

Tessa grabbed Nick by the front of his grubby T-shirt. "Nick, you get in this car. Now." Everyone, Nick included, knew you had no choice but to obey Tessa when she got that intense look in her eye. I loved her for this, except when I was the one she was bossing around. She had that look now, and stared at Nick until he stopped resisting.

Nick pulled himself up onto the side of the car, ready to do a cool-kid move and slide into the backseat in one smooth motion. Instead, he toppled headfirst into the car, with his holey boots straight up in the air.

I could hear his gasp of surprise, then he flipped himself over and into the seat so we could see his face, his knit cap pulled sideways and covering one eye. He was blitzed.

"You guys, you might want to put up the roof," Nick said, adjusting his hat, and pulling it down around his tangled black hair.

"Dammit, is it starting to rain again?" I felt for raindrops with my open palm and looked up at the dark sky. Not a star in sight.

"No, it's just it will be safe. Safer, you know?" And also, I thought, none of his friends would see him in the car with a couple of not-very-cool women. "Uh, but wait for a second before, before you put the top up, okay? I gotta hurl!" And with that, Nick stuck his head over the side of the car and vomited.

At least he didn't throw up in the Ladybug. Between Nick and his barfing and Stanley and his "oopsies," I had experienced the bodily functions of others way too intimately this weekend.

"Okay, I'm good," Nick said, wiping his mouth on his T-shirt.

I rolled up the windows and pushed the button to put the ragtop up. We watched as it magically unfolded and curved up to the windshield. We were all safe and sound inside, as safe as we could be, anyway, in this dicey neighborhood.

I pulled away from the curb. "Where to?"

"We certainly can't go back to my house," said Tessa. "Way too much drama there after the scare with Izzy tonight."

"Let's get some coffee in you, Nick," I said. "And maybe some food. When was the last time you had something to eat?" We headed away from the University District and soon found a diner by Tessa's shop, away from the chaos of The Ave.

As we got out of the car, I noticed Nick seemed to have sobered up a little. He wasn't teetering around quite so much and was able to look at me without his eyes glazing over.

"Oh, Nick," Tessa said, reaching out to hug him. Nick pulled away, and didn't say a word as we walked down the street toward the café, its cheery lights glowing in the darkness ahead of us. A waitress behind the counter waved us in, and told us to take any table we liked.

We stopped at a red U-shaped booth and Tessa tried again. "We are so sorry about Misty. If there is anything we can do..." Tessa reached out to Nick. This time he let her hug him.

Tessa and I scooted into our places on the seat across from Nick. He was looking down at the table, not saying a word, staring at the artificial gold flecks swirling around on the ivory-colored Formica tabletop. All we could see was the top of his scruffy black knit cap. We couldn't see his face or judge how he was feeling. Drunk and miserable, was my best guess.

The waitress moved slowly toward us. There was no rush to get anywhere in the middle of the night. Not for her. Not for us. She pulled a pen from behind her ear, popped the cap off with her gray teeth, and then stood there poised with the pen above her order pad. She couldn't talk because she had a pen cap in her mouth.

Nick hadn't looked at a menu, so Tessa decided she'd order for him. "Okay, I'll have an English muffin and two eggs over easy. My friend here will have your special breakfast with three eggs, toast, hash browns, and bacon. And he wants coffee. Lots of coffee."

The waitress looked at me expectantly.

"Pancakes." If I was going to be awake at nearly one o'clock in the morning, I might as well enjoy myself.

The woman popped the cap back on her pen, and was able to talk again. "Okay, and you, young man, how'd ya' like those eggs?"

"Scrambled." Nick finally looked up at us. His eyes were red. Maybe he'd been crying, but more likely, he'd been smoking more than cigarettes.

"She's all I had." Nick rubbed his eyes, and pulled off his cap. His dark hair stuck up in all directions. I noticed a small geometric tattoo on his wrist. It matched Misty's. I swallowed hard to keep the big lump in my throat from growing bigger. Nick sat there looking at his hands, fidgeting.

"The cop said they aren't going to try and find her killer. He said Misty was killed over drugs, but other than weed, we were clean, and had been for a while." Nick was scraping something out from under one of his nails, and then another.

"Nick? What's that you're picking at?" asked Tessa.

"It's bead release. Last time Misty was dipping mandrels at the studio, I accidentally tipped over the jar and got bead release everywhere. I'm still trying to get it all out from underneath my nails."

I remembered Misty had been dipping mandrels when I was at the studio; I'd watched them clean up the spill.

"The white powder under Misty's fingernails wasn't meth, like the detective suspected, it was just bead release!" I shouted, a little too loudly. The only other customers in the diner, a young couple sharing a piece of pie at the counter, stopped their conversation mid-bite and stared at us. I dropped my volume by a few decibels. "One reason Detective Grant thought Misty was killed in a drug deal was because she had white powder under her nails. He thought it was meth."

"But Jax, why does it matter?" Tessa pressed her palms to her temples, hoping to squeeze some logic into her brain.

"Because if Misty wasn't killed over drugs—and I'd say she wasn't, and Nick, you don't think she was, either—" Nick nodded in agreement, "then we need to look for someone else. Like someone from the bead shop, someone attending the WEED party." Saying "weed party" made me imagine a much different kind of event than a party where a bunch of middle-aged women danced to New Wave hits from a few decades ago.

The food arrived. It took longer for the waitress to bring our meals to us at her snail's pace than it had taken to cook them. I hadn't realized how hungry I was until I started pouring syrup over my perfectly golden pancakes. Yum.

Nick started shoveling food into his mouth.

"Nick, here's the thing. The detective thinks I had a reason to kill Misty," said Tessa, looking at Nick seriously, waiting for what she was saying to sink in. "In other words, if she wasn't killed over drugs, then I'm at the top of the suspect list as her murderer."

"What?" Nick was stunned. "You were so cool to us. You helped us."

"Detective Grant says that because I gave you both free studio time to work at the torch, you and Misty owed me money."

"What? There is no way you'd kill Misty. This is bull—"

"He accused me of trying to kill Rosie, as well." Tessa was trying to keep a steady voice, but I could tell it was hard for her to continue.

"That's easier to believe. That woman was a bitch." The waitress came by and sloshed more coffee into Nick's cup. He picked it up and drank deeply. I could tell he was feeling better, the color coming back to his face. "Did she die? Because she deserved it."

"No, Nick, she's okay, and let me give you some advice," said Tessa. "I wouldn't go around saying things like that when there's a murder investigation going on."

"Although you'll have to get in line to be at the top of the suspect list. Following close behind Tessa is yours truly," I said, as I held up my cup in a mock toast.

"Nick, maybe you could call the detective and tell him about the bead release under Misty's fingernails. It might put him on the right track," Tessa suggested. "And maybe you could tell him you think I wouldn't have harmed Misty because I was supportive of you both."

Tessa shouldn't have been telling Nick what to say, because that could make her look even guiltier.

"I don't think that's a good idea," Nick said. "I don't really like talking to cops. They make me kind of nervous."

"But what if it meant the police were able to discover who Misty's killer was? Doesn't that matter to you?" Tessa wanted to find the murderer, and not just to clear her name. She had cared about Misty and wanted her killer brought to justice.

"When you're on the street, people die, and the cops don't care. Finding Misty's killer—it's not gonna happen."

"Nick, is there any reason to think someone you knew killed Misty? How did Dylan feel about Misty?"

"Dylan didn't know Misty much, only from Fremont Fire. She didn't know him as long as I did. I'd only been hanging out with her for, I dunno, like the last year. Can't think of any reason why Dylan would want to kill her," Nick said, mopping up the last of the scrambled eggs with his toast.

"It seems like Dylan's had it awfully hard, too. Did you know him before he started working with Tessa?" I asked, hoping Nick might tell us more about Dylan and Tracy.

"Yeah, he had some girlfriend a few years ago. She disappeared, I guess. I met him on the street back then. He was kind of trashed for a couple of years. Dylan, he had family around, but they kicked him out. And he hung out with me for a while."

"And then I hired him at Fremont Fire," Tessa said, thinking about when she'd opened her studio a few years ago. "When I first started, he'd come by and just look in the window. I eventually invited him in, and had him do some work for me, hauling oxygen tanks around, and lifting heavy boxes of equipment." Tessa was a softie for any hard-luck case, so it made sense she'd wanted to help Dylan. "I'd give him a few dollars for his work."

Nick continued talking about Dylan. "He has skills, you know, working at the torch. He used to make us these killer pipes with boro." Boro was borosilicate glass, the kind of glass used to make pipes for smoking pot, but also good for making beautiful beads and sculptures. Nick and Misty worked with boro at Tessa's studio, and were able to coax the most beautiful colors out of the glass to make their gorgeous beads.

"Right, and when he started working at my studio, I wouldn't let him make pipes, so he started to make beads. His ability to work with glass in the torch was amazing. He showed me things I'd never seen anyone do in boro." Tessa was proud of how much she'd helped Dylan. "I'm glad I could hire him as my studio assistant. With his apartment, it seems like he's on the right track. If he can just start selling his beads, he'll really be in good shape."

Great shape, as long as he hadn't killed anyone.

TWENTY-SEVEN

I FELL INTO MY BED just after two. I wasn't going to be able to continue with these late nights, not without experiencing a serious meltdown. I fell asleep thinking of Gumdrop and his psychic powers. Although deep down I knew he didn't have any such thing, I wished I had him here with me now. I could use his psychic powers to help me figure out who needed to strangle people to solve their problems.

Based on what Nick told us, Dylan didn't have any reason to want to harm Misty. As for Dylan's relationship with Tracy, Nick didn't seem to know much, other than how devastated Dylan was when he and Tracy broke up, which we already knew. We did learn one important thing from Nick: Misty didn't have meth under her fingernails. Knowing Misty wasn't killed in a drug deal gone bad narrowed the list of potential killers, although it did mean the detective would likely continue to scrutinize Tessa. I hoped Nick might change his mind about talking with the detective, especially if Tessa was about to be arrested for murder.

I was exhausted but couldn't seem to settle down. I slept fitfully, tossing and turning. Something was bothering me, but I couldn't piece it together. Like a necklace, I wanted to organize all the pieces and string them onto a thread, one bead at a time. But some of the beads were missing.

When I woke up in the morning, I felt like I'd slept about half the hours I had been in bed.

I stumbled out to the kitchen to make some coffee.

There was no sign of Marta. Thank goodness, too, since I didn't think I could deal with her. In fact, I wasn't sure there was anyone I could have faced right now.

I had my workshop today. I was prepared and feeling confident. I'd done many presentations when I worked at Clorox, and learned to get over my stage fright (conference room fright?) years ago. I was hoping to appear as calm as Dylan had during his beadmaking demo at Fremont Fire.

While the coffee was bubbling through the coffee maker, I filled a bowl with cereal. I looked into the bowl, and then realized I wasn't hungry. At all. It dawned on me that the tall stack of pancakes I'd eaten in the middle of the night now sat in my stomach like a lead weight. Ugh. Even coffee didn't sound good.

I headed back down the hall to the studio. I had the samples I needed for my project, and instructions on how to create my necklace. The necklace was made of seven oval beads, each with swirls of transparent color on the surface and white at the core. Students could also opt to make a bracelet with just three or four beads. Anyone who wanted to complete the project needed to have some smaller beads, some wire, and a clasp. I had hoped to inspire people to try different combinations of colors, and to experiment with how to use my beads in a design.

I pulled the sample necklace I'd be using out of my jewelry box. This one was made of different tones of blue—from a light sky blue, to a denim color, to cobalt, and then to a dark inky blue, all swirled together. With white glass beneath all of the cool blue tones, each of the beads seemed to glow.

My beads. I had nearly forgotten. Allen had my beads last night. And Rosie's, too. I needed to call the detective right away. He needed to know about Allen, and the evidence I'd recovered from him. I grabbed my cell from my dresser and gave him a call.

"Grant," the detective said, as he answered his phone.

"Detective Grant? It's Jax O'Connell. I've got some important news. I found the beads you were looking for." I explained to him what had happened the night before. "I've got them right here," I said as I walked toward the living room.

I looked on the coffee table for the baggie I'd put the beads in last night after I'd gathered them up. They were gone. Oh. No.

"Good job, Ms. O'Connell, I'll send an officer over to pick them up."

"Uh, detective, I think you should wait on that." I'd lost Rosie's beads. Or, more likely, they'd been stolen. Again. "I seem to have misplaced them."

"What? Please, Ms. O'Connell, I'm losing my patience, and I am tired of you wasting my time. If you want to play amateur crime-fighter, do it on your own time. Not mine."

"No, you see, it's not like—"

"When you have some real evidence, please be in touch."

Who could have stolen those beads? The only person who had been here other than me was Marta. Why would she want them? Could she have tried to kill Rosie? As far as I could tell, the two women didn't even know each other. And Misty? I couldn't imagine any reason Marta would have anything to do with her. It was just my wild imagination at work again. I needed to get dressed and stop worrying about untangling this mess.

Some people choose their jewelry to match the clothes they're wearing. I do the opposite, picking my clothing to complement my jewelry. I needed something to go with my blue necklace. I chose a pale blue silk top and black skinny jeans. Val would be proud of my fashion choices, although she would have preferred more cleavage and more sparkle.

I was going to have to find Val and get the latest update on Rudy, although I was hoping to avoid hearing the gory details, which Val always seemed to over-share.

I thought I'd check in with Rosie and see how she was doing before I headed out for the day. I called the hospital.

"Virginia Mason Medical Center," the operator said when she picked up.

"Oh, hello, Virginia," I said, as I hunted through my closet for some cute shoes to wear today.

"Ma'am? This is 'Virginia Mason Medical Center.' That is the name of the hospital, not my name," the operator said in a short, clipped tone. She probably gets to deal with space cadets like me every day.

"Oh, right. Sorry. I'd like to check on a patient. Rosie Paredes."

"It looks like Ms. Paredes will be leaving this afternoon against the doctor's recommendation. The notes in the system indicate we are processing her discharge at this time. Since she is leaving against her doctor's orders, we require that she be released to a family member.

"Her daughter?" I asked.

"It says here that she will be leaving with her husband, Rudy Paredes."

Husband? Rudy? Was Rudy's last name Paredes?

I pressed the End button on my phone.

Rosie didn't have a husband. Or did she? I found Rudy's business card. Paredes Painting. What the heck did this mean? One thing it meant was that Rosie wasn't a single mom. But if she was married to Rudy, why hadn't I seen him at the shop? Were they divorced? Maybe. Did it mean that Rudy was Tracy and Benny's dad?

There were too many questions, not enough time, and frankly, not enough brainpower to figure out anything, given my lack of sleep during the last few days.

I tacked Rudy's card to the corkboard, right next to a picture of Gumdrop. His green eyes stared back at me from the image.

Green eyes. Who has green eyes? Not Rudy. Not Rosie. Not Tracy.

I called Tessa's land line, and Ashley answered.

"Hullo," she said.

"Hi, Ashley. It's Jax."

"Uh-huh," Ashley said, surly in her lack of interest.

"Can you do me a favor?"

"Um, I guess," she said, continuing with her tone of apathy.

"Is Benny awake? Can you tell me what color eyes he has?"

"Uh, yeah, he's watching cartoons. Lemme check." She dropped the phone. It sounded like it hit the floor. I heard a commotion, and an "OW." I hoped she hadn't forced Benny's eyes open to check them. She came back and said, "Green. Or, sort of greenish-blue."

"Thanks, Ashley. Nice talking with you," I said.

"Whatev." I heard an abrupt click. Ashley wasn't in the mood for idle chitchat.

Benny's eyes were green, in a family of people with brown eyes. What were the chances of that? From what I understood about genes, somewhere between slim and none.

I knew someone with green eyes. A person. Not a cat.

TWENTY-EIGHT

I CRUISED SLOWLY through my neighborhood looking for Gumdrop, and then drove to Aztec Beads, making a small detour to get coffee, since I'd skipped my cup at home. Tracy was searching for some silver wire on a display rack when I came in.

She looked tired, her eyes smudged with makeup and tears. Maybe this wasn't the best time to quiz her about her family, but I wanted to talk with her before Rosie showed up. I hoped I would see Rosie at some point this morning, because I wanted to find out if her husband Rudy was the same Rudy who was going to paint my kitchen. Oh, and the same Rudy who had been watching movies, and doing who knows what else, with Val, just to make things more complicated.

"Hello, Jax," said Tracy. Her tone was dark. Clearly, she had not gotten over the fact that she'd found me snooping around on the balcony the day before.

"Tracy, hi, listen, I hope you're not still upset about yesterday. I was, and still am, trying to figure out who strangled your mom and who killed Misty. You've got to believe me," I pleaded with her.

"I want to believe you, Jax, but I'm just having trouble figuring out who to trust right now."

"I get it. I really do."

Tracy had found the sterling wire she was looking for, and she fidgeted with it as we talked. Her long hair fell across her face as she released a rattling sigh. I was running out of time, Rosie would be here soon. If I was going to talk with Tracy about her family, it was now or never.

"Tracy, I need to ask you about something. Or someone."

"Dylan?"

"I saw how you reacted when you saw Dylan here in the shop, and I noticed how you disappeared from Fremont Fire when he started his demo. I figured it was because of him, but I wasn't sure why. Dylan told me yesterday you two were together nearly five years ago."

Tracy set the wire down on the counter. She stretched one hand across her body and rubbed the opposite shoulder, giving the odd impression of an empty embrace. Tracy looked up at me. Her eyes were filled with tears.

"You didn't seem too happy to see him," I said.

She sniffed. "I just hadn't seen him in so long, it was a shock to have him standing right in front of me."

"It sounds like he's missed you a lot."

"Jax, I know you're trying to help, but seriously, this is all a bit complicated."

"But, Dylan is more than just your ex-boyfriend, right?" I asked.

"How did you know?"

"For one thing, everyone in your family has brown eyes, except Benny." All those years of college biology had taught me that green eyes didn't usually show up when both parents had brown eyes. "And then there was the fact that you disappeared about five years ago."

Tracy looked at me and swallowed hard. I knew the truth, and she couldn't deny it.

"Benny, he's just about the right age. Did your mom take you away because you were pregnant?"

"Jax, look, you figured it out. Good for you. But you just need to forget that you know anything about this. My mom, she can't find out that you know. Okay? She'd kill me if she knew I told you."

"And Dylan, he doesn't know, does he?"

We looked out the window and saw a pickup truck pull up to the curb. It was sporting a bumper sticker that read, "May The Force Be With You."

Too late. Tracy and I would have to finish our conversation later.

A man got out of the truck, came around to the passenger side, and helped Rosie onto the curb. She slapped him away, like a bothersome mosquito. Rosie was definitely bouncing back.

It was Rudy—at least, it was someone who bore a close resemblance to Rudy the housepainter.

Rosie's face looked puffy. She hadn't been able to put on any makeup to help with the purple circles under her eyes. I think she had hoped to sneak into her shop and upstairs without anyone noticing.

Tracy had regained her composure, standing up taller and brushing back her hair. Lara, or Sara, came over, and Tracy handed her the wire she needed for the class. Back to business-as-usual, for now.

"Mama, what are you doing here? You're supposed to be in the hospital," Tracy said, as Rosie and Rudy entered the shop.

"I was done with that place. They said I was okay, no damage. I called Rudy and had him come and get me." Rosie was still wearing her clothing from the other night, including the beautiful sash she had been wearing around her waist. She had artfully wrapped the scarf around her neck to hide the bruises she'd sustained when the necklace had been pulled tight.

As Rosie adjusted the sash, I wondered if she could have used it to kill Misty earlier in the evening before her fall.

"Rudy?" I said, trying to get his attention.

"Uh, yeah?" Rudy said, trying to figure out if he knew me. "Oh, right. You're the lady who hired me to paint your kitchen. Jax, right?"

"Rudy, you look different to me," I said, examining him closely.

Rosie took the opportunity while I was focused on Rudy to sneak away to the apartment. She didn't want people in the shop to see her looking sick, and didn't want anyone making a fuss.

"Yeah, Val cut my hair, shortened up the sideburns, too, you know, made me look real good," he said, checking over his shoulder to see if Rosie was out of earshot.

He was right. Val had worked her magic on Rudy. His hair was now washed and short. He looked much better without the long greasy ponytail. The muttonchops were thankfully gone. And his pockmarked face—he now looked more rugged than ugly and mean. Val was a genius at makeovers. No doubt about it, Rudy was a new man.

Before I could start quizzing Rudy about his relationship with Rosie, and the rest of the family, the phone buzzed in my pocket. I pulled it out and saw Andy's name flashing on the screen. I moved onto the back patio so I could answer my brother's call.

"What did you learn?"

"Well, your perp, he's clean."

"What? What are you talking about? Why are you talking like that?"

"Oh, well I thought that's how people spoke when they were investigating a crime."

"I don't know how sleuths talk, but I'm thinking they just talk like normal people."

"Oh, well, yes." Andy was rethinking what he had to say. He must've been practicing that line for a while before he called. Andy, my nerdy little brother, needed some help with his social skills. I guess that's why he was such a good computer programmer. He could sit in his dark office for hours, or days, at a time and never have to interact with other human beings.

I tried again. "So, Bro. Are you saying Allen doesn't have a criminal record?"

"Exactly, Jax. Nothing comes up for him, no felonies, no aliases, no DUIs. Oh, he was married and then got divorced."

I remembered now. Allen's wife was angry that he had broken the coffeepot. You'd think that wasn't grounds for divorce, but in Seattle's coffee-loving culture, anything was possible.

"How'd you find all of this out, and so fast?"

"If I told you, Jax, I'd have to kill you." Those were the last words I wanted to hear. I'd had enough violence recently to last me a lifetime.

I was disappointed. I'd hoped Andy would find something that would help me figure out all of the strange things that had happened this weekend. Why'd Allen steal the beads? Was he trying to protect someone? Was it possible he could have taken the beads to hide the evidence of his own fingerprints?

"You found nothing bad?"

"Nope. An upstanding citizen."

"Thanks, Andy. Sorry for the hassle. I owe you one."

"NBD."

"What?"

"No Big Deal." With that, he hung up the phone. Andy definitely needed to work on his communication skills, and spending his days tied to his computer wasn't helping the situation. I should send Val down to San Francisco to get him out into the world and have some fun. On second thought, no, that was a terrible idea. Who knew what kind of a makeover she'd try to give him?

I came back into the shop, but Rudy was gone. Tracy was ringing up a customer's purchase. I wanted to continue our conversation about her family, but I'd have to wait until the customer was gone.

I spent some time browsing in the store and admiring beautiful strands of Czech glass beads. They were about the size of my thumbnail and flat, with colors swirled together. They reminded me of my own lampworked beads, but these were much smaller than what I usually made. I let the strands fall through my fingers, the light from the window playing off their flat surfaces. I couldn't decide which colors I liked the most: orange with red swirls, turquoise with dark blue, or ruby with white, all perfect combinations.

"Jax?" Judy from JOWL yanked me out of my mesmerized state. "Are you all right?"

"Oh, yes, just looking at the yummy colors of these beads." I hoped Judy hadn't realized I was in la-la land when she had interrupted me, my brain still overloaded, trying to make sense of all that had happened. Those swirling colored beads made me wonder, just what was the perfect combination of motives and people? What combinations existed that I was unaware of?

"Are you ready for your workshop?"

"Ready as I'll ever be." Of all the confusing things that had happened this weekend, of all the stress and heartache, I knew the one thing I could do without difficulty was teach my workshop, especially since there were only going to be a couple of people there. Who would want to see my demo?

Everyone.

TWENTY-NINE

WHEN I WALKED INTO the classroom, I was overwhelmed. Every seat was taken. People were standing at the back of the room. It wasn't a large classroom, but still, I was surprised so many people would be here to support me.

As I looked around the room, Val threw me an air kiss when our eyes met; Tessa gave me an enthusiastic thumbs-up; Marta looked like she was ready to let rip one of her signature wolf whistles. After she saw me shake my head slightly, she took her fingers out of her mouth. Dylan was there and must have sneaked in through the backyard, hoping to avoid seeing Tracy. Allen was nowhere to be found, which wasn't surprising after he'd stalked out of the house last night. Sitting front and center was Frankie Lawton, the jewelry designer. He twiddled his fat fingers at me in a cute, but weird, wave. He didn't look like Santa anymore. Today, he looked more like a Keebler elf, with his yellow tie, red vest, and green jacket.

"Today I'll be showing you how to make a necklace using these lampworked beads that are called 'white hearts,'" I said. "I'll start by showing you how to make each of the wire links for connecting the beads together…"

When I finished the presentation, I received an enthusiastic round of applause that made me feel great. Finishing the workshop freed up my mind. There were many more things to think about.

One of those things was Misty. I couldn't stop thinking about her. If she wasn't involved with drugs, then why would someone want to kill her?

Setting aside the question of *why*, the other big question was *who*. One of us? As I looked around the room, we were all there—could one of us be the murderer? Not Dylan. According to Nick, there was no reason to think Dylan wanted Misty dead. Not Tessa. Not only was she my oldest and best friend, Tessa cared about and supported Misty. Marta didn't even know Misty. Val? Val had been home most of the weekend watching Luke and Leia fight Darth Vader, and was only at the party for a brief time. Frankie? I didn't know anything much about him, and wasn't sure if he had ever met Misty.

It came down to Rosie, who was in the hospital when Misty was strangled, and Tracy, who didn't seem strong enough to kill much more than a fly.

I simply wasn't going to be able to figure out who had been responsible for this weekend's mayhem. Clearly, I didn't have a future as a detective, amateur or otherwise. Fortunately, I thought I had a future as a glass beadmaker.

I went over to my display to speak with the people who had just watched my demonstration. I was glad to see I had a swarm of customers waiting to talk with me, and selecting beads to purchase. Several women had collected four or five pieces and were trying to figure out which ones coordinated best with other beads in my trays. It was fun to see which combinations worked best together, and I was delighted by the choices many of the class attendees had made.

My friends came over to congratulate me on the workshop, but they didn't stay long, wanting to make sure they weren't in the way of paying customers. After everyone had made their purchases, Frankie approached me.

"Your beads and necklace designs are fabulous. Fabulous!"

"Thanks, Frankie."

"What do you have for me?" Frankie said, looking over and seeing my empty trays.

"Oh, Frankie, I'm sorry, I didn't set anything aside for you. I figured I'd have plenty left at the end of the weekend." Ugh! How could I have blown this so badly?

"In that case, I'd like to place an order," Frankie said, whipping out his checkbook. "You have five different color combinations, right? I'd like five of each color. Twenty-five beads. Okay?"

"Wow, Frankie, sure. That would be great. Thank you so much." I was flustered. I had just completed my biggest sale ever.

"Here's my card. Just send them to this address."

"Oh, and Jax, have you seen a girl who makes beads like this?" Frankie pulled a bead out of his man purse. "She seems to have disappeared."

I knew exactly who made beads like that. I had one in my pocket, and Misty had made it. I had a lump in my throat, and swallowed hard. "She's not around anymore," I said, unable to say, "She's dead," knowing what emotions would be unleashed if I had to utter those tragic words out loud.

"Oh, well, if you see her, please give her my card," Frankie said pressing another card into my hand. "I'd like to order some more."

"Ta-ta! Looking forward to working with you," Frankie said, and headed out the door. I stood there leaning against my display pedestal, staring after him, dumbstruck and thrilled beyond words.

As I watched Frankie leave, I saw something else equally surprising: Dylan and Tracy standing at the front counter. Neither of them were running away, each one watching the other intently as they headed out the back door and onto the patio together.

Tito ran by me, carrying a hank of beads in his mouth. What an obnoxious little dog. "Tito! Drop those beads," I said, wondering if he'd actually obey me. Tito dropped the beads, and growled at me. I turned to gather my things, and I felt Tito bite into the hem of my pants.

"Tito! You ungrateful mutt. I saved you from prison, and you treat me like this?" I said, shaking my leg until he let go. Tito scampered

off. I'd seen him grab the cuff of Frankie's red trousers at the party.
At the time I hadn't thought anything of it. But now I remembered
what Frankie had said:

I don't know why Rosie doesn't keep Tito under house arrest.

Frankie knew Rosie. And he had one of Misty's beads, so he
knew her too.

I was going to have to talk with the detective and suggest he
consider Frankie as a suspect. Or, maybe I shouldn't say a word, and
just chalk it up to my over-active imagination once again.

For now, I needed to get out of here. I headed home, hoping for
some peace and quiet. The weekend was almost over, and I'd be glad
when everything got back to normal.

THIRTY

I PARKED THE LADYBUG behind my house, unloaded the car, and brought everything inside. It felt good to be in my studio, and I had work to do. I needed to make 25 beads for Frankie. That was cause for celebration. I'd have enough money to paint the kitchen walls, and maybe Rudy could give me a quote on painting the cabinets as well, which would go a long way toward making the kitchen look like it wasn't about to be shut down by the health department. That is, if Rudy ever got around to giving me a quote. What about Rudy? Was he really married to Rosie? How did he fit into the rest of this strange weekend and its events? I could grill him when he got here to do some painting, someday.

I heard a quiet knock at the studio door.

When I opened it, my neighbor, Mr. Chu, was standing there, and he was holding Gumdrop!

"Mr. Chu, you found my cat!" I hugged Mr. Chu. I hugged Gumdrop. Then I hugged Mr. Chu again for good measure. He didn't seem to like me hugging him.

"Didn't you realize you had an extra cat?" I asked.

"I wasn't sure," he said. "I've got a cat that looks like this one, and I thought it was him, until I saw them both together."

Sheesh.

"And you know, he's a nice cat. If you ever decide you don't want him, let me know, because I'd take him off your hands," Mr. Chu said.

"Yes, I will certainly keep that in mind."

Not in a million years.

"Thank you. Really," I said.

"You know, if you love your cat so much, he should be wearing a collar," the old man said, scolding me. "You wouldn't want him to get lost and end up at the pound."

"You're right, Mr. Chu. You are so right. Thank you again." I reached out to hug him again.

I was overwhelmed with joy. Other than the sales I'd made today, this was the only good thing that had happened all weekend.

"All right, all right." Mr. Chu wasn't one for a lot of emotion. He waved his weathered hand over his shoulder as he walked away, the belt from his ratty robe dragging on the ground. Through a break in his curtains, I could see several pairs of cat eyes watching him through the window as he crossed the alley back to his house.

"Oh, Gummie, you are one lucky kitty that Mr. Chu found you!" I said, hugging him. "And, I am one lucky person that Mr. Chu found you!"

I carried my darling cat out to the kitchen. As I passed by the guest room, I noticed the door was closed. I could hear Stanley snoring inside the room, or at least I assumed it was him.

I set Gumdrop down on the kitchen counter. "Let me see you, you fluffy fur-ball." He hadn't been gone long, but I felt like I needed to make sure he was okay. It seemed like he'd gotten plenty to eat at Mr. Chu's.

"Come on, Gummie," I said, looking at him and hoping for a psychic connection, "Can you tell me who murdered Misty? How about Rosie—do you know anyone who would want to kill her?"

Gumdrop stared at me, and then he looked down at his empty food bowl.

Nothing. So much for my psychic cat.

I gave him some crunchy food. Unimpressed, he sauntered off.

Even if I couldn't figure out who killed Misty, I should at least be able to figure out the mystery of the missing beads. Where was that baggie of beads I'd confiscated from Allen last night? Not on the coffee table where I thought I'd left them. Not in the catchall basket of beading magazines and half-finished jewelry projects next to the sofa, and not on the Oriental rug. I'd have to ask Marta about the beads when she returned.

I settled myself into the studio to start work on Frankie's special order. I pulled the last batch of beads out of the kiln. They were the ones I'd made when Allen was here, in Allen's favorite colors, and mine: purple, blue, and green. What was I going to do with these? I didn't want them. Maybe I could sell them on eBay and get them out of my life.

I started up the kiln, and turned on the exhaust system. Then I turned on the oxygen tank and flipped the lever that supplied the natural gas to the torch. My equipment was ready, and now I needed some glass. I chose my color palette. First, I needed white for the centers. Then, I needed all the transparent colors that reminded me of gemstones: ruby, amber, amethyst, sapphire, and emerald.

I put on my glasses and lit the torch, adjusting the oxygen and natural gas to the right mix so that it was perfect for melting glass. As I was making my first bead, I heard Marta come in through the front door.

"Jax, I'm back!" Marta yelled from the entry.

"I'm in the studio, getting ready to make some beads," I shouted back.

Marta wandered back to my studio and watched me work at the torch for a while.

"Hey, Marta? Have you seen a baggie of beads that I left on the coffee table?" I asked.

"There are bags of beads everywhere around here. I'm not sure which beads you mean."

"It was a special set of handmade beads—they belong to Rosie Paredes. I thought I left them in the living room, but now I'm not sure what happened to them."

"Oh, Jax, I've been wanting to give this to you," Marta said. "It's a little thank-you gift for letting me stay here."

Finishing the bead, I gave it one final twirl in the torch's flame. I put it in the kiln to cool, and turned off the torch. Marta handed me a striped cotton pouch.

"Thank you," I said, pulling open the bag's drawstring. Inside was a basset hound bead. A glass Stanley.

"I hope you like it. It's one of my favorites. Sorry it's not a cat bead, but I'm not very good at making them. Every time I try and make a cat, it just ends up looking like an ugly dog."

"It's fantastic, Marta. Thanks."

"I'm glad you like it," Marta said, beaming.

Gumdrop cruised into the studio.

"Your cat! He's back! Oh, Jax, I am so glad he's okay," Marta said.

"My neighbor found him and brought him over a little while ago. I'm happy to have him back," I said.

"Well, I better go take Stanley out for a little run before he has any more accidents. I'll be back in a little while."

Marta walked down the hall and opened the guest room door. Stanley burst through the door, excited to be going out. His toenails skittered around on the hardwood floor, and the tags on his collar jingled. Marta clipped Stanley's leash onto his collar and they headed out the door.

I wanted to check on Gumdrop and make sure he hadn't flown the coop again, now that he had seen, or at least heard, Stanley.

"Gumdrop! Here kitty-kitty!" I called. As I walked by the guest room door, I remembered something. When I was searching for Gumdrop, I'd looked under the bed and had seen a dog collar with tags on it. If Stanley was always wearing his collar with tags, then what was that collar doing under there? I had to check. It felt weird going into Marta's room—well, it was *my* room, in *my* house, so I thought it was okay to go in there, although it still felt like I was violating Marta's privacy. I got down on my hands and knees and felt around under the bed. I found what I was looking for, and pulled it out.

It was a small collar with a tag on it. "TITO" it said on one side.

"If found, please call Rosie Paredes."

Tito's collar.

Marta. What had Marta done? Taken Tito's collar? I'd found Tito at the pound with no collar on. How did this fit with what had happened this weekend? I hadn't a clue.

Marta came back into the house. "I forgot to bring the poop bags." I was standing in the hallway with the collar in my hand.

"Marta, why do you have Tito's collar?"

"Oh, I'm doing a special order for Rosie. She's excited that her sweet little doggie is getting a pretty necklace."

Marta slipped by me into the guest room to find the poop bags, and I went back to my studio—trying again to think about work, and to enjoy melting glass, to return to normal where people didn't get murdered, and where there were no obnoxious dogs, or obnoxious owners. I heard Marta moving things around, trying to find the poop bags. Her room was a mess, so it didn't surprise me that it was taking some time for her to find anything.

"Okay, see you later," Marta called, as I heard her shut the front door.

I worked at the torch for a while. Melting glass was a good thing to do when I needed to meditate. The dancing flame and the gentle movement of the molten glass calmed me, and allowed me to think.

I thought about how I'd come so far in these last few years. I'd made many new friends and built a home for myself here in Seattle. I'd come a long way, and not just in the number of miles I'd travelled to get here. I thought about my trip here, with my travel buddy Gumdrop asleep beside me, on our cross-country adventure. I remembered the giddiness I'd felt as I whipped through Post Falls, Idaho, and finally crossed the state line into Spokane, Washington.

Rosie and her family had been living in Spokane these last few years. It was just another insignificant detail that ultimately didn't matter, at least as far as I could tell. I wished I were able to take the smallest details and turn them into solutions, like Sherlock Holmes.

Post Falls...Sherlock. Where had I heard that before?

Ellison's Post Falls Sherlock Stanton. Also known as Stanley.

Marta was from Post Falls, Idaho, just a few minutes from Spokane.

I was sure that meant that Rosie and Marta knew each other.

Marta was involved in this weekend's mayhem. There was no doubt about it. I turned off the torch, and decided to call Detective Grant. He needed to know there was something strange going on. I was certain Marta had taken Rosie's dog.

What horrible things was Marta capable of doing?

I found my phone and pressed Detective Grant's number on the recent calls list. The number rang and rang, and then flipped over to voicemail. He probably saw I was calling and decided not to answer, not wanting to hear my latest wacky theory.

I left a simple message. "It's Jax O'Connell. Please call me. It's urgent."

"Hellloooo!" Val called, letting herself in, which she had recently started doing without any encouragement.

"Val? I've got to talk with you. I need help figuring something out," I said, heading down the hall. "I just couldn't get away from the idea that Tito's collar somehow fit into the strangulations.

"Oh Jax, darling, it smells funky in your kitchen. Have you been trying to cook again? Well, not to worry, because I brought us a snack. Biscotti and Sauvignon Blanc."

When I got to the kitchen I realized what Val was talking about. It smelled terrible. But not like food, like skunk. And not like skunk, but like natural gas. I smelled gas—the front of the house was filled with it.

"Val! Val! We've got to GO!"

"But, we need to—"

"No no no! Time to get out of here!"

"Really, because—"

"Dammit Val, out the door *right now!*" I grabbed her arm and pulled her toward the door. Her high heels were striking the floor as we ran, and I hoped they wouldn't make a spark. If they did, we'd be blown to bits.

We ran out the door, Val still holding the plate of biscotti and her bottle of wine. We left the door open with the hope that some of the gas would dissipate. Gumdrop immediately ran out the door, and headed for Mr. Chu's. At least I knew where I'd find him later.

We stood across the street, trying to figure out what to do.

"Call 911," I said.

THIRTY-ONE

"**I'M ON IT.**" Val pulled a rhinestone-covered phone out of her pocket. Since her nails were too long for her to use her fingertips, she used a knuckle to press the keypad.

We sat down on the curb and waited for the fire department to arrive, hoping we were not about to witness Seattle's largest fireworks display, when my house, both halves, was blown to smithereens.

"Biscotti? Wine?" Val suggested, completely ignoring the severity of the situation. "Sorry, no glasses, unless you want to risk going back inside." This was what I loved about Val—she never took anything seriously. Even though she might be about to witness the destruction of everything she owned, it didn't seem to bother her, as long as she could have a glass of wine while it happened.

"It's okay, I can drink right out of the bottle," I said, taking a swig of tart white wine followed by a bite of biscotti.

"What did you say was in this cookie?" I said, choking, and wondering why it tasted like Clairol Herbal Essence shampoo. I swallowed the dry chunk of biscotti and washed it down with more wine.

"Oh, it's got some rosemary from our front garden, and you know, some anise, and a little bit of mint. I added some extra to give it a kick." I hoped it was real mint and not Gummie's special catnip. And I wished Val would stop experimenting with her recipes.

Fire trucks arrived, followed by two police cars, an ambulance, an emergency response vehicle, and the hook-and-ladder engine. It was an impressive response to our crisis.

"Hunky firefighters," Val said, nodding in their direction as they piled out of their red trucks.

"Oh, yes," I said, taking another bite of cookie, which didn't taste any better than the first bite. I sat there wondering if my house was going to go up in a giant KABOOM, and knowing there was nothing I could do about it. I'd just have to trust the firefighters would do all the right things.

When a police officer approached, we told him we could smell natural gas, and that it smelled like it was coming from the stove in the kitchen. I said I hadn't cooked anything since the day before, and that I didn't think my houseguest had done any cooking, either.

My houseguest. I looked down the street and saw Marta rounding the corner. "There she is now," I said.

Marta saw all of the fire engines, and then she saw me sitting on the curb. She turned and started to run in the other direction, poor Stanley trying to keep up on his short basset hound legs.

"Do you think she has anything to do with this?" the officer asked, since running away was usually considered a suspicious activity.

"Yes, I think so," I said. "I definitely think she has something to do with this."

It was easy for the cops to catch up with Marta—she was middle-aged woman with a dog who couldn't run without stepping on his own ears, and they were two fit 30-year-old police officers. They were driving their police car, so that made the race even more unfair.

They caught up with Marta, and we could see her talking and waving her arms around excitedly. The police officers were equally animated. They were too far away for Val and me to hear anything. We could see poor Stanley watching the conversation like a tennis match, his head moving from side to side as he listened to each person yell at the other.

They put Marta and her dog in the back of the police car, and then drove toward us. One of the officers rolled down his window. "We're taking them in for questioning."

"Them? You are seriously going to take the dog in for questioning?" I asked.

"No, actually, we were going to drop the dog off at Animal Control until we can figure out whether to keep Ms. Ellison in custody."

"What? No! You can't take Stanley to Animal Control. He'll die in there!" squeaked Marta, from the backseat of the cop car. "He's a pure-bred dog, a champion, not some dirty mutt."

"Not some mutt like Rosie's dog?" I asked her.

"Rosie didn't deserve to have that dog. She deserved to lose everything!" Marta yelled, coming unglued right before our eyes. "I wanted to take everything she loved. Her dog. Her store. Her daughter. Everything!"

"Her daughter?" I asked, my head swimming, taking this all in. "You wanted to take her daughter away from her?"

"Rosie has everything—a family, and a perfect life here with her new shop. Me, I have nothing," said Marta, tears welling up in her eyes. "She needs to know what I feel like, having lost what I wanted most."

"Marta, I lost my cat for a couple of days—and I have to say it was terrible to have lost something as precious as a pet," I said.

"Animal compan—"

"Shut up, Marta. Look, I lost Gumdrop, and it hurt so much. Imagine how you'd feel if you lost Stanley."

Marta gasped for air, and then said, "I can't bear to think of it."

"Then think of Rosie."

"That bitch stole my dream. Stole it right from underneath me."

"How'd you know Rosie?" I asked. "How'd you get to the point where you wanted to hurt her so badly?"

"I worked with Rosie in Spokane at the Godiva Call Center. You'd think working for a company that was all about chocolate would be heaven, right? Well, it wasn't. It was just like any other stupid job, and I hated it. All I wanted to do was get out of that God-forsaken place," Marta said.

"Every day I'd look online for the perfect place to live and work—a place where I could open a dog-supply shop and doggie spa," she continued. "I had the perfect dream, to find a cute little neighborhood where I could sell my dog necklaces, with an upstairs apartment, and a yard where my dog could play. I found my perfect place in an online ad, and I showed it to Rosie on my laptop during one of our lunch breaks."

"Rosie's shop? Rosie's apartment?" I asked.

"It was supposed to be *my* shop. *My* apartment," Marta said, wrapping Stanley's leash around her hands and pulling it tight. "When I decided to come here this weekend, I thought maybe I'd discover that the place wasn't that great, and I could feel better about what happened."

"But didn't Rosie notice you at the shop?"

"I wasn't at the shop until the party. Besides, when she saw me, she knew I was a beadmaker, so there was no reason why I shouldn't be there. And I told her there were no hard feelings. That, of course, was a big fat lie."

"And me? Why try to kill me?"

"You'd have figured out about Tito's collar, as soon as you talked to Rosie. She would've told you she didn't place a special order, and then you'd have known the only reason I had the collar was because I'd taken it off Tito when I dropped him at the pound. Then Rosie, and everyone else, would know what I was up to. It was perfect. I realized I could just leave the stove on in the kitchen. You were back there, working in your studio. You'd light your torch, and BOOM, you'd be gone. It would look like a studio accident. Easy. No one would suspect a thing."

"Ma'am, we need to take this woman down to the police station. It seems like we have several things to talk about with her," said the officer in the passenger seat, bending his head low to look at me out of the driver's side window.

"Jax, Jax, I beg you," Marta called to me. "Take Stanley, please. Help me in just this one way. I know I shouldn't have done these things. I couldn't take it. Rosie had taken so much away from me, I just wanted to see how she would feel to have what she loved taken away from her."

Val piped up. "Let the dog out. I'll take care of him until this is all settled."

"Thank you," said Marta, wiping the tears off her cheeks.

The officer opened the back door and let Stanley out. Then he got back in the car and drove away.

We could see Marta's face staring sadly out of the back window as the police car got smaller and smaller, and then disappeared from sight.

"So, Stanley. I guess you're going to be with us for a while," Val said, reaching down and giving him a vigorous scratch between his two floppy ears with her long nails. Stanley's eyes closed as he enjoyed the attention.

"Us?" I asked.

"Well, you know, joint custody. I wouldn't be taking him if you hadn't had the bad judgment to invite a crazy killer into your house."

Stanley was listening to us, and wagging his tail. He *was* kind of cute, but I was sure Gumdrop would hate him.

"And dogs—guys love dogs. Dogs are guy-magnets." Val said, trying to convince me. I wasn't buying it.

Just then, a cute firefighter came over. "Your gas has been turned off. Looks like you left your stove on," he said. I knew who had left the stove on, and it wasn't me.

"Thanks," I said, finally relaxing now that I knew my house and all of my belongings weren't going to explode.

"Nice dog," the fireman said, as he reached down and gave Stanley a gentle pat on his side. "What's his name?"

"See? See?" Val whispered in my ear. "This dog's a magnet."

"Stanley," I answered.

We finally were able to go back inside the house. We went into the kitchen and poured our wine into glasses.

"So, Val, I have some news," I began. I needed to broach the subject of Rudy gently. "It's about Rudy."

"Oh yes, Rudy. Doesn't he look amazing? I think he looks so handsome now that I've cut off his icky ponytail and cleaned up those long sideburns. He looks like someone I could date."

"See, that's the thing. Rudy's married. I'm pretty sure."

"Oh, no he's not. You see, I've started to ask every new guy I meet that question."

"Val, I'm not sure you'll always get a truthful answer," I said. "I mean, really, what guy who wants to go out with you is going to say 'yes, as a matter of fact, I *am* married?'"

"I've gotten a variety of answers, and at a variety of levels of truthfulness," she admitted. "But, here's the thing. Rudy *did* answer me, and it was the weirdest answer I've ever heard, and believe me, I've heard a lot of strange answers. Rudy said he wasn't actually married, but sometimes he pretends to be."

"What?"

"It's super-sweet. He said he does it as a favor for a friend. In fact, when I talked to him a while ago, that's what he said he'd done today—helped a friend get out of the hospital, because they wouldn't let her leave without a family member."

"Well, I think I know who the friend is. It's Rosie."

"Thank God he's not married to Rosie," Val said, taking a large gulp of wine.

"I'll drink to that."

THIRTY-TWO

THE PHONE RANG around 9 on Sunday morning. Fortunately, I was already up and drinking coffee at the kitchen table, with plans to take Stanley over to Tessa's to romp around with Joey in the backyard for a while.

I recognized the number; it was Detective Grant. I pressed the Answer button.

"Good morning, Detective," I said.

"Good morning, Ms. O'Connell."

"What can I do for you?" It was hard to believe that a week after the murder at the bead shop he'd need to follow up with me, on a weekend no less.

"I thought you might want to know there's an excellent article in the *Seattle Times* about you and your glasswork." The detective's voice was missing the snarl I'd heard in it before. Off the clock, he seemed like a different guy.

"That's terrific news. I wasn't sure when it was coming out." I'd have to run out and grab the paper after I got off the phone. For now, I had a few questions for the detective.

"Can you tell me what happened with Marta?"

"She confessed to murdering Misty Carlton—a case of mistaken identity. Apparently her target was Tracy Paredes," the detective said. "Marta saw a young woman in the darkness on the patio the night of the party and thought it was Tracy. Ms. Ellison said she had some 'dog necklaces' in her purse. Does that make sense to you?"

"As a matter of fact, it does. 'Dog collar' is probably a better description."

"She used one of those collars to strangle Misty, and then threw her in the Dumpster."

"That's what I had pieced together from what she said before the police officers took her away," I said. "She wanted to take everything from Rosie; it was just hard to figure out how Misty fit into that."

"We've also charged Marta Ellison with the attempted murder of Rosie Paredes. In Ms. Ellison's confession, she said she showed Ms. Paredes an advertisement for a property for lease in Seattle, and that Ms. Paredes had beaten her to it, by renting the property the same day," the detective explained.

"Rosie stole what Marta desperately wanted," I said. It was hard for me to believe that Marta, or anyone, would kill because of a piece of property.

"Precisely," the detective said. "Oh, and you didn't hear any of this from me, right?"

"No, Detective Grant, you didn't tell me a thing."

"Oh, and you can call me Zachary."

I was on a first-name basis with the stern detective? This was an interesting development.

"And you can call me Jax."

We were quiet for a moment. And then the moment grew into an awkward silence.

"Okay, Jax, well, I should be going."

"Thanks for calling, Zach."

"Zachary, never Zach," he corrected.

The detective, even when trying to be nice, was a little prickly around the edges.

"Maybe we'll run into each other again someday."

"I hope so," said the detective, and then hung up.

I hope so?

I tip-toed barefoot out to the curb to get the newspaper. Since it had been raining all night, and I didn't want to get my slippers wet, I'd left them inside. This made sense to me, but it's hard to explain why.

I flopped down on the couch, and Gumdrop curled up next to me, kneading his paws into my thigh.

"Ouch!" I said, as I removed Gumdrop's sharp claws from my PJ bottoms.

I found the article in the *Arts and Leisure* section. The article was, in a word, wonderful. Allen had done a terrific job explaining how glass beads were made, and about the difference between artisan-made beads and those made in China that are churned out by the thousands. The article had great things to say about me, and my work, and the images Allen had chosen were brilliant. I couldn't believe it. I figured I'd blown it, after having accused him of stealing beads and watching him march out of my house.

My cell phone rang. It was Allen. I answered, not knowing what else to do. I suppose I could have let the call go to voicemail, but I was curious.

"Jax, it's Allen."

"Yes, Allen, I saw it was you calling." I was trying to stay calm, cool, and collected. The last time I'd seen him, he was making a fast escape from my house after I'd confiscated some beads from him.

"I have something for you. Can I stop by?"

"Sure. Give me about 30 minutes?" I needed to get out of my jammies and either fluff up or glue down my hair. I was pretty confused about Allen at this point. He'd written a great article about me. It made it difficult to be mad at him, and hard to believe he was angry with me. I was confused, but I figured I'd keep an open mind and see what happened.

Allen arrived a half-hour later, and Stanley and I greeted him at the door. Gumdrop was sitting on the kitchen counter, a place he'd discovered where he could be safe from Stanley. Of course, he also hoped he could score some catnip from time to time by sitting there.

"Hi," Allen said, grinning when I opened the door. He seemed to be pleased with himself. He looked down at his dripping boots. "Let me take these off, so I don't get your floor all wet."

"Good idea." I was playing it cool.

"Can we go out to your studio? I want to show you something, and I think it would be best where the light is better." It was true, the studio had terrific light, with huge windows on the side and at the back.

When we got into the studio, he pulled out two fancy packages from his bag. "The first one is for you," he said, gently placing a fiery red box in my hands.

My coolness was fading. It was hard to be mad at someone who was giving me presents. "Should I open it?"

"Yes, of course!" he said, eager to see my reaction to what he'd brought.

I removed the silky white ribbon and pulled off the lid. Inside was a beautiful bracelet, made of my beads.

"But, I don't understand, I took these away from you—you stole them."

"I didn't steal them, I took them so I could keep them safe. I found your bracelet broken on the balcony—I think it must've broken while you were struggling to help Rosie." Allen was trying so hard to be sweet, to explain that he'd meant well. It would've been better for him to have given this crucial evidence to Detective Grant, or at least explained his plan to put the jewelry back together. Then again, if the detective had analyzed the fingerprints on the beads, he would have been accusing me of strangling Rosie, because my fingerprints were all over her beads.

If I took it to its ludicrous extreme, I could say that because the beads were missing, the detective didn't take me into custody. By not being in custody, I was able to discover not only Misty's murderer, but the person who'd tried to kill Rosie, as well.

"But how'd you get them back after I confiscated them from you?"

"Oh, easy. Marta. She's one tricky woman. I had her sneak them back out of the house." Yes, I thought, she was tricky in many ways.

I recalled asking her where the lost baggie of beads was, and she never had answered the question. Instead, she'd distracted me by giving me a glass basset hound.

"Don't be mad, okay? I was trying to be nice," he said, earnestly.

"But how'd you know how to string them?" I asked. I put on the bracelet. It was perfect.

"I watched one of the demos this weekend, of course. It was supposed to be a weekend of education, right? Well, I learned how to string a bracelet and a necklace." Allen was proud of himself. What a great guy. I could definitely feel my coolness melting away.

"And this one," Allen said, opening the larger black velvet box tied with a red ribbon, "is for Rosie."

"Oh, Allen, it's magnificent. You put it back together exactly how it was before." It was Rosie's special collection necklace, with the different beadmakers' beads flowing together in one long strand.

"I hope you don't mind, but I put one of your beads in Rosie's necklace, too. You have one less in your bracelet than you had before. But I thought she'd like to have one of your beads, since you saved her life."

"I don't mind at all." I was touched. How sweet of him. I reached out to hug him, and he'd decided he wanted more than a hug. He wrapped his arms around me and gave me a kiss. It was a fantastic kiss. Wow.

We heard Stanley hacking and coughing, and trotting toward us. When Stanley got to the studio door he dropped one of Allen's beautiful leather boots, now covered in dog spit and teeth marks, on the ground at our feet. And then he coughed up a piece of boot leather that landed on the top of Allen's foot.

Immediately, Allen's mood changed. The sweetness was gone.

"Goddamn it!" Allen yelled. Stanley turned and ran down the hall, careening off the walls.

Allen picked up the slobbery boot and headed back down the hall, cursing the whole way to the door.

"Where are you going? Look, I'm sure Val will pay for your boots, or I can. Wait!" I said, following after him.

"You know, Jax, you seem like a terrific person. But I've got to say, this situation is crazy. Dogs eating my boots, your psycho cat attacking me, you accusing me of stealing—this place is a loony bin!"

He stood at the front door looking pathetic, holding one boot in his hand. The other boot was nowhere to be found. Stanley had probably taken it off to a secret lair to chew on later.

"I love my life, every single crazy bit of it," I said, opening the door wide. "If you can't have a sense of humor when things go wrong, then you shouldn't be here."

"But I…" he gestured with the boot in his hand, frantically looking around for any sign of his missing footwear.

"Out."

He left, carrying one boot as he walked gingerly down the front path in his stocking feet. In the rain. Poor man. Bad man. At least I'd figured it out sooner, rather than later.

I found Stanley back in the guest room with his head on top of Allen's other boot. I reached down and gave Stanley's head a good scratch. "Good boy," I said. His heavy tail gave a few good thumps on the floor in appreciation.

I needed to get over to Aztec Beads as soon as possible. I had Rosie's fabulous necklace, and I knew she would be overjoyed to see it again.

I hopped into the Ladybug and headed over to the shop.

Rosie was standing at the front counter when I came in the door.

"I want you to have this," I said, handing her the elegant black box.

"Oh, Jax, what is it?"

"Open it and see," I said, urging her on.

She opened the box and was silent for a moment.

"Oh, my goodness," she said finally. "It's perfect. I never thought I'd see these beads again. I figured they were gone forever."

"I didn't do it. Allen did," I said, feeling like I should confess that I hadn't put the necklace back together. "He learned how to string beads this weekend."

"That's wonderful. I'll have to thank him next time I see him." It might be a long time before we see him again, given his exit from my house a little while ago.

"And look," I said, "he fixed my bracelet."

"Such a quick learner, and a nice guy, too."

"Let's just stop at 'quick learner.'"

Rosie looked at me now, her expression softer than I'd ever seen it.

"Jax, thank you for helping me. I know I've not always been the easiest person to be around." Understatement of the century. "I'm going to try and relax and not be so bossy, and I'm going to trust Tracy to take on more responsibility here at the store. I don't want to destroy my family, or my business."

I had a few dozen questions for Rosie, about Benny (her grandson?) and Rudy (her husband?), but those questions could wait.

I went over to Tessa's and brought Stanley along. I figured Joey could give Stanley a good run around the backyard. The poor dog only had Marta his whole life. He seemed to enjoy playing catch with Joey, and Benny, who was over for a play date.

"So, it turns out Marta confessed to killing Misty, and trying to murder Rosie," I said to Tessa, sipping my coffee. We were sitting out on her back porch while the sun streamed down on us through the tall pine trees in the yard.

"Marta had her perfect dream—to live in the apartment upstairs and run her pet shop, sell her dog necklaces, have a grooming area where the gallery is now. And live happily ever after.

"In fact, that was going to be the name of her shop: 'Happily Ever Arfter,'" I said.

"Arfter?"

"Yes, get it? It's a play on words."

"I get it, but it's too cute for words," Tessa said.

"You mean cuter than 'dog necklaces?'" I asked.

"Yes, just about that cute," Tessa said.

"But Rosie beat her to the punch. She got the place, and rented it right out from under her friend."

"Not nice," said Tessa.

"No, not at all," I agreed, "but at least Rosie didn't go around murdering people."

"I wish we could get Rosie to lighten up. I wonder how?" Tessa asked.

"I talked with Rosie earlier, and I think she's going to try and relax."

"You know, working with beads can be soothing," Tessa said. "She's got a shop full of them. Maybe she'll make a necklace from time to time."

"Any news on Nick?" I asked.

"Amazing news," Tessa said. "Frankie Lawton got in touch with him, and Nick's going to make some beads for him in the style Misty used to make."

"Terrific."

"And, Nick's been sleeping on the couch at Dylan's apartment lately, and he's going to start helping him with the rent."

"That will definitely help Dylan make ends meet," I said.

"How's everything working out with Stanley?" Tessa asked.

"Val is completely smitten. She says she's given up men for Stanley."

"We'll see how long that lasts," said Tessa, with a laugh.

"Well, I've also got the challenge of getting Gumdrop and Stanley to like each other. We are somewhere between mild loathing and indifference.

"They're not getting along?"

"It's much better than it was. Before, it was a full-scale war."

"And how's your kitchen looking? Did Rudy finish painting?"

"Geez, he's taking forever. He seems to like to come over and work each morning, then take a break in the afternoon when Val comes home from the salon. They finished watching all the *Star Wars* movies, and have been on a *Star Trek* binge lately. It's making me crazy."

"*Star Trek*? Val just doesn't seem the type," said Tessa.

"I couldn't agree more. But, I'm getting the neighbor-of-Val discount, so I can't complain."

We heard a knock on the front door. "Come on in," hollered Tessa.

It was Tracy. She walked through the house and sat with us on the back porch. We watched the boys and the dog rampage around the yard.

"Tracy! Tracy! Look at this ball!" Benny handed her a wet and slobbered-on ball. "I threw it! The dog gave it back to me!"

"Cool. You want to throw it to him one last time?"

"Yay!" Benny threw the ball as far as he could, and Stanley went running after it.

"Okay, kiddo, let's go. I have a special friend named Dylan I'd like you to meet. I think you're really going to like him."

"Is he nice?" Benny asked.

"He's terrific, and he's looking forward to meeting you."

"Someday I need to tell you about Tracy and Dylan. And Benny," I whispered to Tessa.

"What—"

"Shhhh. Don't ruin the moment."

And with that, Tessa and I looked at each other, clicked coffee cups, and smiled as Tracy and Benny walked hand-in-hand out the door.

ACKNOWLEDGMENTS

It takes a village to write a book. Thanks to all the amazing villagers who read, reviewed, and edited mine: Lori, Jennifer, Sharon, Pam, Leslie, Phyllis, Jim, and Deborah. An enormous thank-you to Jeff and Kiera for their support, patience, and love. I couldn't have done it without you.

ABOUT THE AUTHOR

Janice Peacock decided to write her first mystery novel after working in a glass studio full of colorful artists who didn't always get along. They reminded her of the quirky and often humorous characters in the murder mystery books she loves to read. Inspired by that experience, she combined her two passions and wrote *High Strung*, the first book in the Glass Bead Mystery Series featuring glass beadmaker Jax O'Connell. Janice has continued the series with *A Bead in the Hand*, and *Be Still My Beading Heart, A Glass Bead Mini-Mystery*.

When Janice isn't writing about glass artists-turned-amateur-detectives, she creates glass beads using a torch, designs one-of-a-kind jewelry, and makes sculptures using hot glass. Her work has been exhibited internationally and is in the permanent collections of the Corning Museum of Glass, the Glass Museum of Tacoma, WA, and in private collections worldwide.

Janice lives in the San Francisco Bay Area with her husband, two cats, and an undisclosed number chickens. She has a studio full of beads...lots and lots of beads.

CONNECT WITH JANICE PEACOCK

www.JanicePeacock.com
jp@janicepeacock.com
www.blog.janicepeacock.com

Sign up for Janice's newsletter:
www.tinyurl.com/janpeacnewsletter

www.facebook.com/janpeac
Twitter, Instagram: @JanPeac
www.pinterest.com/janpeac
www.JanicePeacockGlass.com
www.etsy.com/shop/janicepeacock

Did you enjoy this book?
Please write a review on the website where you purchased it.

MORE BOOKS IN THE GLASS BEAD MYSTERY SERIES

A BEAD IN THE HAND
Glass Bead Mystery Series
Book Two

A bead bazaar turns bizarre when jewelry designer and glass bead-maker Jax O'Connell discovers a dead body beneath her sales table. Suspected of murder, Jax and her friend Tessa scramble to find the killer among the fanatic shoppers and eccentric vendors. They have their hands full dealing with a scumbag show promoter, hipsters in love, and a security guard who wants to do more than protect Jax from harm. Adding to the chaos, Jax's quirky neighbor Val arrives unexpectedly with trouble in tow. Can Jax untangle the clues before she's arrested for murder?

BE STILL MY BEADING HEART
A Glass Bead Mini-Mystery

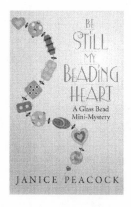

It's Valentine's Day and Jax O'Connell's red VW bug is missing. Did she forget where she parked The Ladybug as she rushed to deliver her handmade glass beads, or has the beloved car been stolen? Searching the streets of Seattle, Jax and her best friend, Tessa, face some unsavory characters. Jax regrets not having a date on the most romantic day of the year after spotting Ryan, Seattle's newest—and hottest—cop and running into Zachary, the stern yet sexy detective. She must take matters into her own hands to find The Ladybug and salvage her love life, and do it before the day is over. This stand-alone short story features the quirky characters of the Glass Bead Mystery Series and is available as an ebook.

Find retailers for the Glass Bead Mystery Series at
www.janicepeacock.com/books.html

OFF THE BEADIN' PATH
Glass Bead Mystery Series
Book Three

Glass beadmaker Jax O'Connell and her friend Tessa have no idea what challenges await them when they take a glassblowing class with Marco De Luca, a famous Italian glass artist—and infamous lothario.

After the first night of class, Tessa sees a body through the rain-streaked window of the studio. The next morning there's no sign of Marco, and one of the studio owners is also missing. The local sheriff isn't taking the disappearances seriously, but Tessa knows what she saw. To complicate matters, Officer Shaw and Detective Grant are both vying for Jax's attention as she tracks down clues in a small town that's been keeping more than one secret.

Jax and Tessa must face their fears to find the body and uncover the killer before another life is shattered.